RIN OGAWA

A Cat's Promise: Secrets of The Kingdom

ETERNITY ZERO PUBLISHING

First published by Eternity Zero Publishing 2024

First edition

ISBN (paperback): 979-8-9924117-0-6
ISBN (hardcover): 979-8-9924117-1-3

This book was professionally typeset on Reedsy.
Find out more at reedsy.com

Contents

1

A Cat, A Book, and A Promise

A long time ago, there was a place hidden within the deepest forest of a forgotten land. This place was teeming with magic. The plants, animals, and all the land's inhabitants were blessed with its power, especially those born under the blue moons.

This place in the long-forgotten woods became a legend to those who dared to enter, as they would never return again. It was given the name Caillte, the human word for "lost."

As the decades passed, this land evolved, and before long, decades turned into centuries. The stories of the forgotten woods were but whispers in tales told to children by the humans who lived outside of the wall of trees that encased those woods.

Like any society, there was a hierarchy, and I was born into it. My father, the great Cyrus Silver of the royal house Silver, was a prodigy, like his father before him and his before that. He was born under the bluest moon of the era, his skills matching

1

none. He was the greatest mage ever to rule Caillte, and I, Leona Silver, was the biggest failure ever to disgrace the royal family.

My father, being the greatest, meant there was much pressure to measure up as his only heir. My magic was less than adequate; I was the first child born with crimson hair in a line of the perfect trademarked gray hair of the Silver family. Not to mention the heir to a kingdom that traditionally passed from father to firstborn son. My father says I took after my mother; she was said to be even more fearsome than even the purest forest-born mage; she had hair the color of the sun's rays and eyes like the deepest part of the forest.

I don't remember her, but sometimes, when he talks about her, I feel like I know her. I'm 17, which I'm told is "but one step closer to inheriting the realm," by the royal court and servants. In Caillte, you become an adult the moment you bear the crest of your family house; traditionally, this crest is passed to heirs on the eve of the winter solstice following their 17th birthday. And this winter, I am to assume my crest. Caillte is my home, and it's my future. These castle walls will someday be mine to rule over if I can ever get a handle on my magic.

"*Purr*" A nudge on Leona's arm tore her from her thoughts; it was her partner in crime, Mars. She was a stark black cat with perky ears and an eye for mischief; she was also Leona's oldest and dearest friend. "Mars, how am I supposed to write my biography when you keep purring on me?" She said with a huff. "*Who was I kidding? I'll never be queen.*" she thought to herself as she leaned back against the window seat and looked around her room. The stone walls were pale gray and adorned with silk tapestries, and the window was open for the breeze to come in.

The sun's soft light danced over her as the leaves from the tree cast little shadows when the breeze moved. Her red hair softly tousled. Leona often wondered what it must be like to be one of the people in town, to make their own destiny, to leave the forest, and to see what's outside those walls. Mars softly nuzzled her as she pet her gently, and in her daze, she thought of blue eyes, like the sky, and felt the blood rush to her cheeks. "Dean," She breathed.

Her father would never approve. He wasn't born here like the others in Caillte. He was left on the edge of the forest 17 years ago. Even though he was raised amongst the knights of the forest, he was always viewed as more of an outsider than anyone else. Despite being human, he gained abilities that were more impressive than those of the average mage within the walls.

Dean was a tall young man with pale blue eyes and thick black hair. His smile was kind, and he treated everyone he met with the utmost respect. Leona's eyes turned to the window; her chambers overlooked the training grounds for the knights just outside the gates. It took no time for her to find him sparring among the others.

Dean's movements were laced with a fierce intensity, precise and swift. Each swing of his sword was a practiced ease. The strain of his muscles against his tunic was a reminder of the tireless dedication and years of determination that he had put into becoming a knight. She continued to observe the training as the head of the knights. A statuesque man with straw-colored hair and kind eyes approached. Leona could tell even from the distance that it was Sir Mikail. He appeared to be joining the sparring match. He wasted no time taking his stance and meeting each of Dean's blows with resounding force as their swords connected. She could not deny that Dean was a skilled warrior; even so, he remained effortlessly kind.

"Oh, Mars," Leona held her above her as she lay on the window seat, her hair gently cascading around her. "I wonder what it's like out there." Mars let out a soft yawn; she was so carefree.

Knock knock, Leona jolted up, and Mars straightened herself next to her. "Didn't I tell you to prepare yourself for the courts?" Coldly exclaimed Yara.

She was an uptight, petite woman who never had a blonde hair out of place; Yara was the head of the court as well as the one tasked with overseeing Leona's upbringing and preparation for her future. Yara was beautiful underneath all her stringent behavior and rigid posture. Her blonde hair fell at her shoulders delicately in small waves, and her eyes were a deep blue, like how she imagined the oceans she read about would look. She had skin the color of parchment without a sign of age. *"She must be the same age as my mother,"* Leona thought to herself as she let out a sigh in response.

"What's wrong with what I'm wearing?" She gestured to herself, begging the question. Yara looked Leona up and down, looking more offended as she went from her black boots to her tights and dark green dress that fluttered ever so slightly above her knees.

"Royalty doesn't dress like the common folk. Have you no shame? I'll have the servants prepare something appropriate while you comb that wild bush you call your hair."

She quickly slammed the door; Leona supposed her frown probably only added to her sense of urgency to make her into a "real lady." Her mess of long, wavy crimson hair was never quite tamable. She wore it down with her bangs tucked behind

4

her ear, exposing her crescent moon earrings and alabaster skin. She looked at herself in the mirror and saw the fire in her hair and the same forest in her eyes that she imagined her mother had.

Just as quickly as she had lost herself in thought, she was pulled back out by the sound of scurrying as the maids entered her room in a flurry of satin, garnets, jewels, and shoes.

"Lady Silver, Yara has chosen your attire for the court," Sylvie said. Sylvie was a tall woman with olive skin and intense eyes. Her hair was braided tightly around her head. She held in her hand a corset gown adorned with golden threads and delicate jewel flowers. The gown was the softest white, and the flowers were every color of spring.

She was enveloped in satin before she could utter a word in protest—tug...*tug*. She gasped with each tug of the lace, binding the corset. Just as quickly as it began, she was placed in front of the mirror once again; this time, however, the reflection, looking back, did not remind her of her mother. It reminded her of what she was expected to be. Her crimson hair was tightly bound by a silver pin, jewels hanging from her pale neck, and a dress that looked fit for a ball rather than everyday life.

"Your father is waiting," Yara said flatly as she pulled her toward the door in a flurry of satin and steps, the servants piling around them. The castle halls were magnificent stone, and windows as tall as the ceiling gave the perfect view of the forest and the life teeming outside those walls. The sun's rays touched the floors ever so slightly as they walked, casting shadows with every step. A rebellious strand of hair slipped out from Leona's pin, daring to make Yara scowl. She turned her eyes ahead as the large auburn doors opened; a cacophony of color and flowers filled her vision; the throne room was like spring in a shell. The walls were adorned with silk tapestries depicting stories of the greats, flowers on every mantle daring to reach the sun, and the most beautiful view. Her father's throne sat amongst all this, where a small pond trickled next to his throne, housing some of the fish that called the forest springs home.

"Leona!" a booming voice exclaimed; before her eyes could adjust to the light and colors of the room, she was embraced by a firm hand. "Father!" His smile was soft and sincere. He was a large man with broad shoulders and a strong frame. His silver hair fell perfectly at the nape of his neck, and his eyes were the color of slate. *"Father was every bit as regal and kingly as you could imagine."* Leona thought to herself.

"I have wonderful news!" he proudly exclaimed with a smirk. "In six weeks, I am arranging your coronation. I've spoken with Yara, and we both agree that there is no time like the present. We've been expecting you to prepare for this day since you were born, but I think the only true way that you will really gain control of your magic is to be in the moment." He beamed a large smile. He was certainly proud of his idea.

All the color drained from Leona's vision as he continued to speak slowly, guiding her alongside him as he talked and gave commands to the servants simultaneously. She continued to smile and nod as her father expanded on his idea of her undergoing the coronation. He had so much faith in abilities she had no control over.

"At the end of the ceremony, you will take the oath as I did and bind yourself to the forest. All will be perfect!" She looked at him with shock, and she could see his expression waver as he sensed her hesitation. "Leona, you won't disappoint me...will you?" he asked quizzically.

"N-no, father. Of course not," she muttered. "It's just that the winter solstice isn't for another 12 weeks..." The words escaped her lips quietly as she lowered her eyes so as not to catch his gaze. "Leona Sivine Silver, the solstice is when you will inherit our family crest; the coronation is for inheriting the crown." His words were not sharp, but they were stern and firm. Leona was no stranger to her father's demeanor; he was the king, after all, and who was she to question his divine ordination?

"Of course, father," Leona muttered, defeated.

"Great! Yara, you must summon the court..." his voice faded as her thoughts became overwhelming. "*How was I supposed to complete a spell to bind myself to the forest, a spell reserved for the most talented mages, when I couldn't even complete a spell to spark a fire or flower a tree? I'm doomed.*"

Leona politely excused herself and hurried back to her room. Yara was occupied with her Father, planning what would undoubtedly be the worst day of her life. She crashed onto her bed, and her hair exploded from the pin that bound it. Hot tears burst from her emerald eyes.

"Meeeoowww" Mars nuzzled Leona gently as she cried, feeling the weight of a future laid out for her that she had no choice but to fulfill. She gathered her knees to her chest, her hair streaming around her in waves. "Mars, I'm going to be the laughingstock of the entire land. A ruler with no magic in a place where it's everything..."

Mars had little sympathy as she pulled at the hem of Leona's gown with her teeth. She was yanking her towards the window. Her eyes caught a flash of stark hair walking below. "The answer is so clear! Thank you, Mars!" Leona jumped up quickly, pulling on her boots and grabbing her bag; Mars jumped inside as she slung it over her shoulder and promptly opened her

7

windows. The breeze blew her gown and hair; on the side of the castle, Ivy vines grew thick and long, forming a lattice of greenery all the way down. She quickly grabbed on and began to climb down. She had climbed this ladder of vines many times growing up. It was the only way for her to escape the prying eyes of servants and be alone.

"A Princess should be quiet, collected, and obedient, after all." Yara's cold words rang out in her memory as she made a defiant face to shake them from her mind. She continued to climb down, the wind tickling her face, and each hair gently dancing with the breeze. Her eyes sought the flash of dark hair that had inspired this reckless idea.

Thump. As she jumped to the ground, the dust settled quickly around her. Leona broke into a sprint around the corner, and there he was, sitting under the oak tree that overlooked the village contained within the castle gates.

"Dean," She exclaimed between breaths. He quickly came to his feet to steady her; his hand gently clasped her waist as she began to stumble. He tilted her chin up so she would meet his eyes. *"They were the most beautiful shade of blue."* She thought to herself.

He quickly untangled himself from her and looked away, touching his hand to the back of his head and clearing his throat. "Leona...I mean, my lady. Um. To what do I owe this surprise?" He asked without meeting her eyes, "Is your father aware you're unaccompanied out here?"

"Of course, I'm on official business, actually..." She lied, averting her eyes; Dean let out a sigh.

"You're a terrible liar, Leona." He looked at her up and down. "Did you run away from one of Yara's dress-up sessions?"

"No! It's not like that!" She exclaimed, feeling the heat rise to her cheeks. Leona turned around swiftly.

"You're still the same loudmouth you were when you were a child." Dean smiled softly.

Leona recollected the many days spent sneaking out of her quarters to try and leave the palace gates; on one such occasion, she ran into a boy with hair the color of onyx and piercing blue eyes.

Dean was abandoned on the edge of the forest, and as such, the others in Caillte did not take kindly to a mere human being allowed to stay in the forest. Almost as if destiny had acted on his behalf, he obtained powerful abilities out of thin air and could use magic just as well as those born within the forest.

Leona was forbidden from seeing Dean on her 15th birthday, as she was to be the next ruler of Caillte; she had no more time for childish play, and Dean was not worthy of standing by the side of royalty as a mere human, even if he was a knight of the forest, according to Yara.

"I am not a loudmouth!" she huffed

Dean let out a genuine laugh before ruffling Leona's hair.

"My apologies, Your Highness. Would you be able to find it in your heart to forgive a lowly knight such as myself?" he said with a playful grin.

"Y-yeah, it's fine," Leona uttered while trying to hide her blush.

"I am eternally grateful. Now, to what do I owe the pleasure of your company?" He asked

"Oh, um, well, you see, father has these plans, and...you were born without magic, right? You were a human, weren't you?" The words escaped her lips before she could even think. Leona quickly put her fingers to her lips as if to stop them from coming, but they had already managed to slip out.

9

Dean looked at Leona, surprised. "Yes, I was born in the human village. I wasn't born with magic. Why do you ask?" He looked at her intently, certainly puzzled by what Leona had just asked of him.

"How did you learn magic?" She blurted out. A look of realization passed across his face, and a gentle smile tugged at his lips.

"Leona, are you asking me to teach you magic?" he coyly asserted.

"Well...I mean...yeah?" Leona quickly explained the urgency behind the request to Dean; he intently listened as she described her lack of magic, the coronation, and that he was her last hope. He was silent for so long that it threatened to tear her apart. When he finally spoke, he pursed his lips and said,

"I think I can help you. But we'll have to wait for the sun to go down; I don't want to risk losing my head".

He made a motion with his finger as if to cut his head off before retreating behind the corner near the edge of the gate, where no one came often, and it was the perfect place to wait out the sun.

Leona remembered the many occasions she was caught with Dean by the other knights or servants. Her father was not particularly fond of them spending time together, nor did he tolerate acts of defiance. She could not help but wonder if her father would punish Dean more severely if they were caught now rather than the times they had been seen as mere children.

The sun fell quickly, and time seemed to escape them. Every moment spent talking about nothing and everything at the same time was a feeling all too familiar. Dean was the closest thing she ever had to the world outside the forest walls, but it was more than that; it was deeper, unexplainable, and all-consuming, and if Leona thought about it too much, she feared she would be swallowed by the very idea of what could be.

Dean was beautiful, she thought as she looked at him. These stolen moments between them were her treasured secret, and she would never divulge it. Nights in Caillte were magical. The forest seemed to whisper, and the sky was the perfect shade of deep violet trickled with silver stars. The only light shone on them was from the moon above, and the lanterns lit with flickering flames.

The castle was no longer bustling as the night descended; a lone guard kept watch, and with the rounds completed, Dean grabbed her cold hand and pulled her alongside him as he led her, quietly sneaking past the many homes and alleyways inside the kingdom to an opening between the gate and the forest. They ran deep into the woods, enveloped by trees and the thick darkness from the cacophony of leaves that threatened to block out all the moon's beams. The only sound in Leona's ears was of twigs snapping as she ran, and her feet became one with the earth beneath them.

Dean abruptly stopped, and Leona halted her steps with him. Mars let out a loud meow in surprise.

"Here." Dean put his hand to the tree's base; beneath his finger was an intricately carved design. He turned his attention to it and began to whisper. The design lit up a pale gold; beneath it, a pattern swirled as if creating a doorway into the ground. Dean used his magic to open it, and before Leona could mutter a word, they fell through.

Leona let out a scream and shut her eyes tightly, anticipating the fall, but there was no crash. She slowly opened her eyes and saw lanterns lighting the walls of a long tunnel. She looked up, and above her were the forest and the stars that they had just been in.

"This is the place Cyrus took me the day I swore my vow to Caillte when I was 7. I swore to protect the forest and the mages within as a knight. It seems like forever since then." Dean released Leona's hand, and she looked on in bewilderment.

"Father brought him here?" she thought to herself, taken aback that she had never known, nor had he ever told her, that he was the cause of Dean's magic.

"What is this place?" she asked softly, touching her fingers along the stone.

"It's the heart of the kingdom," Dean stated and began to briskly walk down the long hall. Leona hurried along with Mars in tow, "The kingdom! What do you mean? I've never seen this before?" Leona stammered.

"That's because it's a secret; only those who have been here before are able to find it," Dean explained. He led her down halls that twisted and turned until they reached a large corridor with an insignia carved on the doorway. Dean turned to Leona and locked eyes with her. He spoke softly, "Are you sure this is what you want?"

His voice was kind but sober. "I know your father can be stern, but maybe if you told him-" Leona cut Dean off.

"It's the only thing I can do. I won't disgrace them again." Leona defiantly stated.

"Leona, I know you and your father don't always see eye to eye, but do you really think he wouldn't understand?" Dean asked, knowing the answer all too well

"My entire life, the only times I have ever seen him is when he wants to address something or discuss my role and who I was destined to be." Her words were laced with a quiet sadness.

12

"I know I'm not the heir he wanted, and as much as I have tried to fulfill that duty, the more distant we seem to drift. I can't ask him; I have to do this myself."

Dean gave her one last thoughtful look before touching his fingertips to the doorway and releasing the same golden light as before. It was as if a veil had been lifted. They walked inside, and surrounding the walls were the most beautifully articulated books Leona had ever seen.

"These are called grimoires. The kingdom keeps them sealed away as a form of protection. The spells that reside inside are forbidden, but they have the ability to grant magic to anyone who reads them and recites the spells within them." Dean looked intensely at the walls lined with books and carefully inspected each one until he stopped at one with vines along the spine. Leona had never seen such a beautiful book before; Dean dared not open it here; he quickly stowed the book within his bag and set off towards the entrance.

"That's it? We just pick a book and go?" Leona asked, confused.

"Not exactly; the spell that was cast here prevents new magic from being cast." Dean quickly took his leave. Leona, in stride, picked up Mars, putting her back into the bag she had slung around her shoulder, and hurried after him.

They quickly reached the hole that had let them in. *"There's no ladder,"* Leona thought to herself. *"How were they supposed to get out?"* And before she had a chance to speak, Dean grabbed her hand and said, "Jump."

They both jumped and as if gravity itself had turned upside down, they landed back upright on the forest floor. The doorway quickly disappeared into little embers of light as if it had never been there.

13

The walk back to the castle was quiet; Leona felt awkward and didn't know what to say. She felt that what she had asked of Dean had become a much greater feat than she originally thought, and she couldn't help but think that she was pulling him into a disaster waiting to happen. Especially if anyone were to find out. The flickering flames of the castle's lanterns shone, and a hand grabbed her waist, pulling her back and covering her mouth simultaneously.

Just outside the line of trees walked the guard in charge of rounds. Her breath caught in her throat. As he continued to lumber by, she stayed as still as a rock itself. Once he was out of sight and the flickering embers of the lantern had turned the corner, Dean loosened the grip around her waist and dropped his hand from her mouth.

"That was close," he whispered. Looking around cautiously.

They quickly scurried back through the gate and around the corner, weaving between the stone homes and buildings of the kingdom's people all the way to the castle and to the vine lattice that climbed the castle walls all the way to Leona's windows. She grabbed hold of the lattice, wrapped her fingers around each vine, and began to climb; Dean was right behind her. She quietly climbed the wall and opened her window as silently as possible so as not to alert the servants in the area. Once inside, she pulled Dean up and into her room. Dean quickly began to use a spell to seal the doorway of Leona's room in case they were to be discovered.

A soft light touched the corners of the room, and a gentle warmth crept over the entire room. Dean uttered "Seal," and the soft light reversed.

"Did you create that spell?" Leona, taken aback, asked Dean, "It's not perfect, but it should do its job," Dean remarked. Leona

14

was more than impressed with Dean. He created a spell all on his own and was even able to control it with simple phrasing and without complicated incantations.

"There's no going back," Dean said as he pulled the grimoire from his bag and offered it to Leona. She looked at the book intently, reaching her hand ever so slowly towards it until her fingers had grasped the leather-bound book.

She gave Dean one last look to reassure him that she was sure, and just like that, the pages began to stir, and the book opened.

2

Curses and Humans

Golden light erupted from the pages, and the air began to stir; before she could contain it, the powers within had become unhinged.

"Dean! What's happening!" She shouted. Dean tried to reach for the book but was thrown back when his fingers grazed the pages. Everything began shaking, and Leona's eyes began to turn the same gold that was erupting from the pages as Mars began hissing. With a loud *whoosh*, the light erupted further, threatening to consume the very room they were confined in. Just as quickly as the power unleashed, the light faded, the wind stopped, and with it, the shaking.

Dean quickly got to his feet and started towards the other side of the bed where Leona had stood before the light erupted. But in her place, only her gown, soiled by the dirt and foliage from the forest, remained, along with her boots and the grimoire, which was slowly dissolving into embers of light.

Dean let out a frantic cry as his eyes searched for Leona. "I–

I'm oka-a-y," Leona's soft voice echoed beneath the bed. Dean let out a sigh of relief, and just as quickly, the panic began to rise in him again as he looked at the pile of clothing. Blood rose quickly to his cheeks this time, and he promptly turned around.

"L-Leona, um, your clothes. Your clothes are on the floor." He heard stirring behind him, and Leona shrieked,

"I'm so tiny! What happened!" Dean turned around, and all the color immediately drained from his face as he locked eyes with her. Mouth agape. However, she wasn't her anymore. She was transformed.

Leona looked at Dean and instantly began to panic. She quickly turned her head to see the mirror next to her, and what looked back was not her. Leona's eyes welled with tears, and she looked at Dean, crushed.

"I'm a cat...I turned into a cat..." she said through tears. Dean ran his hands through his hair as he began to pace.

"Leona...I'm so sorry; I had no idea this would happen." He apologized, defeated.

"I've cursed myself," Leona softly stated as she looked at herself in the mirror. Her eyes remained unchanged, still the same green as the forest; her hair, however, had taken on a new appearance; instead of the long waves she knew, it was now replaced by fur in its place.

"And I'm still ginger..." she cried.

"Leona?" a soft voice called. She turned her head, and Mars looked at her sadly.

"M-Mars!? Did...did you talk?" she asked, utterly shocked.

"Can you understand me?" Mars mused while looking Leona up and down,

"This is insane," Leona sighed, collapsing onto the floor. Mars was empathetic to Leona and did her best to reassure her by lying down next to her.

"It'll be okay," she said gently. Mars knew how hard this was for Leona; she had gone to all this trouble to try and meet the expectations of her father to no avail, and now, Leona was cursed. "There has to be a way to fix this," said Dean, who was in complete disbelief at what had transpired. He frantically began to think and pace. After a few moments of complete silence, so still, it made a pin drop sound like an earthquake, Dean finally broke it.

"If we get another grimoire, maybe we can undo what this one did." Dean was confident that the answer could be found in another book, but before he could finish his thoughts, the sound of shuffling and metal clanking pulled him from them.

A loud *BANG* rang out as the guards attempted to break down the door. Leona let out a panicked cry. "Dean!"

As her father's booming voice pierced through the door, "Leona! What's going on? Guards! Get in her room!" Her father's voice rang out with desperation.

Dean did the only thing he could in that situation: he scooped up Leona and Mars along with Leona's bag. He deposited them inside before slinging it over his shoulder and swinging himself out the window onto the lattice of vines. He quickly slid himself down as fast as he could and dashed for the gates. The guards had gone on high alert, and he noticed the flickering of lanterns headed towards the forest where the entrance to the corridors of grimoires was.

In a snap decision, Dean darted his eyes around to the nearest way away from the castle and commotion and began to run. He ran quickly through the village within the kingdom and broke past the gate. He dashed through the woods, the forest floor breaking beneath him, every step louder than the last, his breath heavy as he ran.

He heard the voices begin to fade as the adrenaline rushed through him, and he fought against the ever-growing fear. Leona and Mars had no idea where they were going; they dared not peek out or risk being seen or worse. Dean ran for what felt like an eternity. When he stopped for a moment to lean against a tree to catch his breath, his eyes caught a faint flickering in the distance. It was different from the lanterns in Caillte. This light was not as lively; it seemed weaker and almost off.

He approached slowly as Leona and Mars anxiously awaited Dean's words; when he broke the line of trees, he was taken aback. It was a human village. Inscribed words on a stone did not look like those Dean knew from Caillte. But there was no going back until he could fix this and undo the curse Leona had fallen prey to.

"Leona? ... Mars?" he whispered, turning his head towards the bag. He slowly peered inside to see Leona's terrified eyes staring back and Mars calmly acknowledging him with an intent look.

"Dean...I'm so scared...if the humans find us, who knows what they'll do," Leona clamored through chattering teeth. She was right. However, Dean didn't know much about the human world, but he did know that magic was confined to the walls of the forest, and humans did not dare enter without attempting to kill any mage they came across along the way. *"What have I done...?"* Leona thought to herself in tears.

"How absolutely incompetent must I be to curse myself?" Dean was so tense; she could feel the panic through the barrier of the bag. *"He must be terrified. And all of this for the sake of helping me."* Leona thought to herself. Mars did her best to comfort Leona with the realization of what they all had done and the

19

consequences of the actions that they were running from. Mars knew as well as Leona that there was no going home this time.

Leona caught a glimpse of the human village through Dean's bag and thought to herself of all the times she and Mars had run to the edge of the forest after a fight with her father; she never dared to go close enough to ever see the humans.

Her heartbeat was fast in her chest, and she felt an immense weight, knowing that this time she could not turn back and see her father reaching out an open hand to welcome her home. This time she had to get it right. She had to fix it.

Dean was careful not to amass any suspicion from anyone who may see them; as the rain sprinkled down, he kept his hood up and collar close to his face. He walked calculatedly and as calmly as he could through the human village towards the open shops and displays.

Human time was not much different than time in Caillte; the concept was the same. However, it seemed that humans were much livelier in the evenings. The sounds, sights, and smells were intoxicating. Dean was careful to keep his bag tightly against him, holding onto the straps as he walked. Fearful of someone grabbing it and Leona with it.

Dean saw soft light flickering from the lanterns and things he had not even entertained as thoughts or possibilities inside the walls of Caillte. However, it was almost as if it was familiar to him, it felt like somewhere he had been before but could not remember. He saw the cobblestone buildings and the small crowd of people shuffling from the inn to the diners and taverns.

The village was alive in the night "Have some boy!" A man shouted slinging his arm around Dean. Dean panicked and jumped back causing the man to stumble a bit. He was not much bigger than Dean and appeared to be tipsy; he had a pale face and dark eyes masked by dirty blond hair.

"Hey! What's your problem!" He sneered at Dean.

"I... I don't have a... a problem," Dean stuttered. The man gave him a dirty look over his shoulder and kept walking. Dean's heart threatened to beat out of his chest.

The village was loud, and he feared the commotion would give them away. He quickly ducked into an open tavern and took the closest seat he could find. It was a large building—much larger on the inside than it appeared.

The building was adorned with beautifully carved wood inside, and the bar was full of chairs. Dean sat in the corner next to a large board on the wall.

"Can I getcha somethin hun?" A smooth voice spoke. Dean met the eyes of the woman before him; she was tall with long, wavy silver hair. She had kind eyes and appeared to be the same age as Leona's father.

"Whateverrr is uh popular," Dean quietly uttered.

"Sure thing, sweetie, I'll bring ya an ale." She left as quickly as she came and made her way through the tavern, winding through the tables back to the kitchen. Dean hadn't noticed before; however, the board wasn't a board at all. It was written in Cailltian as well as human script.

It was a map of the land, and on it were markers and warrants for criminals, quests, magic activity, and the location of Caillte. Dean felt panic begin to rise in his throat. *"These people are exactly like they told us. They'll do anything to get what they want,"* he thought to himself as he looked at the quests.

Quest: *The blood of a pure mage born. 5 Gold Yule.*

Quest: *The tears of a familiar. 1 Gold Yule.*

Quest: *Deliverance of the siren's mage. 1,000 Gold Yule.* More and more all lined up, and finally, the one that made Dean's breath catch in his throat. It was a sketch of Cyrus.

The quest demanded the heart of the king of sinners. And the reward? Becoming the head of the royal knights for the human kingdom. He could hear Leona gasp from the bag. *"How could I have been so stupid...it's not safe here,"* Dean thought to himself.

CLINK: The noise of a mug slamming down on the table pulled Dean away from his thoughts. The frothy liquid sloshed from the sides of the mug. The women hurried off back to other tables, food and drinks in hand. The liquid smelled strong, and Dean had never seen anything like it in Caillte. He gingerly tasted the liquid "Mhhss" he spit it out. It burned and tasted awful. Dean was immediately disgusted; he sighed; he thought the food would at least be decent from what he had heard of the human world, but he thought that they must've been mistaken.

His bag moved ever so slightly, snapping Dean's focus back to Leona and Mars. What was he supposed to do with them? It's not like he could very well take her out in a place like this and expect to be ignored. He carefully looked around; he hadn't seen an area that wasn't littered with people that he might be able to talk to her without drawing suspicion to the bag; then again, everyone in the area seemed rather consumed with the liquid and music.

In one swift motion, Dean pushed himself up from his chair and swung his bag over his shoulder, ducking out of the tavern. The door shut behind him, muffling the noise; he kept his eyes sharp on the street. The night had begun to chill, and rain picked up. The cold drops hitting the ground helped to silence the commotion around him.

An idea came to Dean. He pulled his hood over and gathered himself into a small crook of a building to shield himself from any prying eyes. He pursed his lips and began to whisper. Dean's blue eyes appeared to glow for a moment, like the flickering of a flame. Just as quickly as it started, it had already begun to recede.

"What did you just do?" Leona's small voice echoed from the bag.

"I used an incantation to understand the human's writing. It won't do us any good if we can't read anything." He trudged forward down the winding street, where he happened upon a small building.

Dean felt a rush of pride as he saw the old board that read *Isle Fork Inn*; the sign was old and encrusted with moss. Dean opened the door and stepped inside. The room was dimly lit, and there was an elderly woman who sat behind the counter. She appeared to be half asleep; she had thick-rimmed glasses and salt-and-pepper white hair. She smiled softly at Dean; his hair was wet from the rain, and his clothes clung tightly to his frame.

"You look as though the water washed ya in. Just one?" She mused.

"Yes. Just one. How much?" Dean asked. He didn't have much to offer. In Caillte they trade primarily in goods and services. Dean did have a small pouch of magic-enriched crystals to offer, however.

"For one night it's 1 Yule..." she saw Dean's expression and paused for a moment, "or if there is something of value, I'll take that" she continued.

Dean pulled out the pouch of crystals and handed them to her. Her eyes widened as she saw them,

"Magic!" She exclaimed. Her hand shaking, she hurriedly handed Dean a key with a 3 carved into the handle and a small candle stick lantern.

"Have a good stay, Sir! It's up the stairs to the left." She straightened her glasses and was consumed with admiration for the crystals. Dean considered them worthless in the human world, considering they were almost worthless in Caillte.

The stairs creaked as he climbed them, his wet boots squeaking against the wood. The inn was certainly old, the spindling stairs creaked. The wood was weathered and rotted in parts, and the light was dim from the candles; he rounded the corner, and a number three crudely carved into the door came into his sight. He quickly unlocked it and tucked himself and the bag inside.

The room was modest, with a small bed, a candle and a washroom. It was nothing like Caillte. The room was small, cold, and dusty. "It's safe now," Dean said in what was almost a whisper. Leona cautiously crawled from the bag with Mars in tow. Her green eyes shone against the dim candlelight.

"The human world is awful," Leona said, defeated. Dean could only imagine that she was referring to the wanted poster of her father. Her legs collapsed beneath her from exhaustion; Dean quickly scooped her up in his arms and held her as he sat on the edge of the bed.

"It'll be Okay Leona...I think I know how to fix this," he gently reassured her. She met his eyes, hers filled with tears. "How?" She questioned softly.

"Your father once told me a story of a mage who was once on par with him, he said that Caillte could not contain her thirst for knowledge, so she left to seek the truth in the human world," Dean said thoughtfully.

"If we can find her, she might know how to undo the spell" he continued.

"How are we supposed to find her when we don't even know her name?" Leona said, frustrated.

"I do know her name, Verona the Veracious." Dean clarified. "And I think I know where to look," Dean thought back to the map; he noted that there was an area by the coast that was marked with quests for magic, the only area far from Caillte that appeared to be teeming with activity.

"Back at the tavern, I noticed that the map marked a small town by the sea. There was a quest that wanted someone to find and capture a mage in a place called Siren. It was the only area marked outside of Caillte. She must be there." Leona let out an audible sigh.

"what's the harm in trying?" Mars nuzzled Leona's head in an endearing way. "Fine," Leona uttered the words defeated, as she fell back on the creaky bed. Dean gave her a thoughtful look, the least he could do was find a way to set things right. If it weren't for him showing Leona the heart of the kingdom they would not be in the human realm, nor would she be cursed.

Dean always felt a deep responsibility to Cyrus, and Leona was no exception to that, he would find the answer.

Dean began taking stock of the situation, and Leona's bag spilled out completely onto the bed. The contents of the bag were a jumbled mess of randomness, from torn pieces of parchment to old pens and trinkets. The items they had with them would likely be useless, he thought as he sifted through them. "*Although,*" Dean thought, he began to lay out the pieces of parchment on the bed, forming a crude and jagged square.

"I can work with this" a smile pulled at his lips. Dean turned his eyes to Leona to tell her of his plan, however, she had fallen asleep. Mars gave him a thoughtful look as she lay next to Leona; she ever so gently gestured with the tip of her nose at the blanket, and Dean carefully covered Leona's small form with it.

"I suppose we'll try again in the morning," he whispered to himself, slipping down to the creaky floor below. Dean was determined to keep watch so they could rest easy. Although he lacked his sword, he could do this much. With his eyes piercing the door ahead of him and Leona and Mars resting peacefully on the bed behind, he had a sense of peace.

At the very least, they hadn't been caught yet, by the humans or Cyrus.

* * *

Leona began to stir; her breathing was rapid in her chest. Her eyes snapped open, but she was no longer at the inn. The wind ripped around her in a field of golden grass. The sky was a black indigo above, with a million stars streaking across it.

Leona felt a chill prick her skin, her eyes obscured by a wave of red hair blowing in her vision,

"*I'm human?*" She examined her hands, looking for any clue as to where she was or why she was human again. On her wrist, swirling black vines lined with thorns weaved a mark, the same mark engraved on the grimoire, only a crude, twisted distortion of such.

The mark was embedded in her skin; her fingers frantically ran over it, causing the mark to tighten in response. Leona's breathing intensified as the searing pain on her wrist continued crawling up her arm with the mark in tow, slowly weaving its inky black tendrils up her arm and burning her skin.

A scream escaped her lips as tears began to roll down her cheeks.

26

"My, what a mess you've made," echoed an unfamiliar voice from the darkness. Her tear-stained eyes pierced the darkness around her to no avail. The voice had no form she could see.

"Whose there?" The shaky words fell flat. "Who indeed?" teased the voice. "Please help me! I don't know what this is!" She screamed out to the void in desperation as the mark began to spread again, weaving up her arm; pain began to prick her skin again. Leona's eyes were wide with pain, tears pouring down when the sensation of warmth on the mark snapped her back to attention.

Out of the darkness, slender fingers touched the mark. A sparking hiss began to emanate from the mark, and the black began swirling and receding back to Leona's wrist. The pain subsided slowly.

"Who are you?" Leona pleaded through tears. For a moment, the mark seemed contained, and the fingers that connected to it retreated to darkness.

"Time is short, Cursed Princess. Return to that which is of you".

Leona's eyes snapped open. She sat up quickly, looking around. It was the Inn; she was back. She immediately brought her eyes to her wrist; all she could see was orange fur. She was back, back in this body and in the Inn once again. "*Who was that?*" her thoughts were heavy, along with the sensation of pain still stinging her wrist.

"*It was only a dream*" she continued to repeat over and over. She shifted slightly, catching sight of Dean pushed up against the bed, his eyelids shut, his hair hanging in his face as he slept peacefully. Leona couldn't tell him about this; he would only worry, and that was the last thing she wanted, especially after everything Dean had already done for her. Throughout the years, Dean had always gone out of his way to protect and cover for her whenever she would sneak away from her chambers or hide from Yara's incredulous gaze. She could not bear the weight of solitude as a child any more than he could bear the responsibility of a knight as a child. Dean was kind to a fault, even when he had no reason to be, and she couldn't ask more of him. Mars began to stir; Leona took it as a sign to lay back down and try to sleep. Even if she couldn't sleep, she would feign it.

3

A Journey Begins

Leona often considered herself to be an agent of chaos. However, never by choice. Some way or somehow, she narrowly managed to end up in the center of chaos. This time was no different.

Maps lay sprawled out across the dimly lit room. Dean had tirelessly sought out the discarded sheets of parchment and was attempting to piece them together. Leona and Mars sat quietly on the lumpy mattress. Mars hadn't said a word to Leona since they had arrived, she thought she was lost in thoughts or perhaps upset at the current predicament.

It isn't unlike Mars to close herself up when she is upset and for Leona, she couldn't imagine a thing that would make Mars more upset than what had happened. Dean had been mapping the best way to get to the coastal city of Siren to search for Verona; there were only two ways to do so, he had discovered. It seemed that they would have to travel through the kingdoms' towns and villages, or they would have to travel through the plains on unmarked roads.

Considering the elements and how little Dean knew of the human world, it was a hard decision to make; he opted to travel by way of the kingdom to try to avoid unnecessary and unfamiliar places.

At least so he hoped.

Now that the path was set, all that was left was to gather enough supplies to make it to the next town. Dean's finger ran up the map on the crudely drawn charcoal line he made to a city marked Deorad.

Dean stood up, straightening himself out and gathering the maps along with his belongings.

"I need to get supplies." He said matter of fact.

"How? We don't have any human currency," Leona stated. She looked at Dean questioningly as she sat up on the bed. Mars' ears perked ever so slightly as she listened.

"I have a plan," Dean said slyly. He pulled out a small pouch and poured the contents into his hand. He had found small rocks and pebbles while looking for the maps.

"I don't think the humans will like it very much if we try to give them rocks, Dean," Leona said dryly. Dean grinned, showing his boyish smile, and quickly began to utter something. The room began to stir. "Form." Once he spoke the word, the rocks took on a fiery glow and, with it, a new appearance. As the light faded, magic stones remained—all beautiful and deep with an enticing glow.

"Did you seriously just create magic stones? Why didn't I think of that!" Leona excitedly mused.

"It's one of the first things I learned. Humans seem to like magical items after all." Dean stated matter of fact. He knelt in front of Leona on the bed, gently touching her head,

30

"I'm going to go into town, I'm going to get the supplies, and I'll be back before you even miss me." He smiled and stood up. Leona's heart beat a bit faster.

"Please be safe," she said quietly.

She thought Dean was the best person she had ever known. He was so talented, yet he treated Leona as if she were the most magical person he knew. He was never ashamed of her; he was always ready to help her.

Dean was likely the most skilled knight of Caillte, and his magical abilities were even more remarkable than most of the forest-born mages, yet he never once claimed any praise for it, let alone acknowledge it.

Even though he couldn't have been more than a mere year older than her, he was somehow always so fearless. She felt a twinge of guilt wash over her as he shut the door behind him. Perhaps they wouldn't be in this mess if she had been just a bit smarter, a bit more useful.

Leona had begun to reconcile the fact that the body she was trapped in was but another consequence of her poor planning and an even poorer understanding of magic. Leona sighed and fell backward onto the bed. She stretched her arms above her head. She stared at the ceiling and thought about the type of person that could be useful to Dean.

"You know, I think Dean might just be the nicest human I've met." Mars' soft voice pulled Leona away from her thoughts.

Daybreak had broken, and the soft sunshine shone through the tattered cloth covering the dusty window in the corner.

"Thanks," Leona said sarcastically.

"You aren't a human," Mars teased. She laid herself next to Leona and gave her a reassuring purr. "Things could be worse," she mused.

31

"I'm a cat. How much worse could it be?" Leona whined.

"You could be a mouse," Mars stated as a matter of fact and began to lick her paws and groom herself.

* * *

Dean briskly made his way down the weathered stairs and out the door of the inn. As silent as the night itself, he pulled himself around the corner. The sunrise had been swift, and with it, the town was alive with bustle and work. Dean tried to draw as little attention to himself as possible as he made his way through the streets, carefully looking at the vendors and tents.

A flurry of colors, shapes, and strange objects he hadn't seen in Caillte. Dean thought the humans in the non-magic region outside the forest had such strange customs, from the crude items they used and sold in their shops to the interactions between people. It was so strange yet also oddly comforting.

His first stop was at a stand with canteens of water; he quickly traded a few stones for the supplies and went on to the next.

As he was gathering supplies, he allowed his mind to run rampant. What was he going to do if they couldn't find Verona? He could never face Cyrus again, knowing that he had his only and most beloved daughter cursed.

"Could Cyrus even undo something like this?" Even if he could face the shame, he wasn't certain that Cyrus was even able to help them. There was also the consideration that Leona and Cyrus's relationship wasn't exactly one of mutual give and take. Maybe if he told Cyrus that—*crash*- Dean's shoulder crashed into a tall man in a mesh shirt.

The man straightened, and his steely gold eyes met Dean's.

A shiver of ice ran down his very being.

The man was taller than Dean, with blond hair and a clenched jaw.

"Watch it" the man warned.

"Sorry," Dean muttered. Clenching his supplies and backing away. The man looked at Dean quizzically; he cocked his head, revealing a scar on the side of his face down his neck.

"You lost? You don't look like you're from around here" He sneered. Looking at Dean's clothes, Dean wore a fitted black shirt and worn pants.

"N-no. I'm just leaving" Dean said curtly. Dean pushed himself to move. Out of the corner of his eye, he noticed there was another guy next to him.

"What's that about Aver?" Asked the other man. Taking a bite of an apple.

He was tall with long stark white hair and dull eyes. The second man was in a mesh shirt as well, Dean realized after a moment that they were part of the kingdoms knights.

Dean quickly slipped into the crowd and made his way through the bustle to an alleyway where he rested for a moment. His palms were sweaty. He had never felt so small in the presence of another human. He thought something else must be going on. "I have to get Leona and Mars out of here." He breathed to himself.

He took stock of the supplies he had from the vendors. They could make it; he had a few stones left to trade if they came across anyone on the road to Deorad.

His steps were heavy as he made his way back through the crowded streets and into the creaky door of the inn. The innkeeper had been in her study since they checked in. He had hoped they could avoid her if they left quickly enough. Dean decided that the fewer people they saw, the better, especially after that encounter with the man in the village.

"What was that?" Dean thought to himself. He was told that there was no magic outside of Caillte, but that presence reminded him of Cyrus.

A knight and not just an ordinary human at that. The feeling was unmistakable. The power lurking beneath that human was familiar. It was strong.

Dean decided it would be best he not mention his encounter with the knights with Leona. The last thing he wanted to do was cause her to worry more. The curse was bad enough. He took a deep breath as he stood before the door with its crooked carved 3. He opened it, quickly tucking himself inside. Leona and Mars were both waiting for him.

"Let's get out of here," Dean said, opening his bag and offering it to Leona and Mars. They both agreed and stepped in. He slung it over his shoulder. He blew out the candle on the small table and took one last look. Dean hurriedly shut the door behind them and shuffled down the stairs; pulling his hood up, he slipped back out the door and into the crowd. This time following the path to their destiny. They would go to Siren. They would find Verona. And then they could all go home.

* * *

The light was harsher in the village. The iron mesh clung to Aver's muscular frame. His hair was as golden as the very sun, and his steely gaze matched.

"Help!" Shouted a small woman with frizzy brown hair in tattered clothes. Aver quickly snapped to attention, pushing his way through the crowd. As he forced his way forward and toward the cries for help. He saw a merchant huddled in the corner, wholly consumed by a small glowing stone in his hands.

"My father hasn't moved! Please help," the woman cried as she tried to shake the man out of his trance. He swiftly knelt and grabbed the man's shoulders, and shook him. He forced his head up to meet his eyes, and they were as blank as a sheet of parchment. The man looked onward, clutching the small stone as it glowed ever so slightly. His mouth was agape with a vacant expression.

"Magic stones." Aver spat the words as if they were dirty. He quickly pried the stone from his pale knuckles and crushed it beneath the weight of his iron-clad boot.

The sun illuminated the kingdom crest on his shoulder. As if pulled from his trance, the man stumbled forward into the arms of his daughter. The stone smashed, and with it, the magic had been released.

"Searel," Aver beckoned over a tall man with long, stark white hair and dull gray eyes. His thin frame loomed.

"There's a mage here," he stated. In a swift motion, Aver stood up and began making his way back through the crowd, where others were making a commotion. He followed the noise to an old building. *Isle Fork Inn* was inscribed on an old wooden board above the door. Aver made his way inside; it was dark, all except for the light of a waning candle coming through the window of a small study off the entrance.

He opened the door slightly and saw an elderly woman slumped over a chair, repeatedly rubbing some crystals in her hand. Like the merchant, the innkeeper was completely entranced by the small stones. Aver quickly grabbed them from her, crushing them with his iron-clad hand.

As if a fog had been lifted, the vacant look in her eyes faded, and her mouth no longer sat agape. He knelt by the old woman and questioned her gently,

"Who gave this to you?" She straightened her glasses with a shaky hand

"thhe the boy with the raven hair and hood...he had no yule..." she stammered. Aver instantly pictured the same man who crashed into him in the marketplace that morning. He clenched his jaw. "Where is he?" He growled. "Rr-room three" she uttered. He briskly pushed his way out of the study and marched up the creaking stairs. The moment his eyes caught sight of the carved number three on the door, he had just as quickly kicked it down in one fell sweep.

The room sat empty.

The bed was disheveled. The tattered curtain was drawn. The room was devoid of any trace of visitors. All but for a torn piece of parchment that had snagged on a rusty nail in the door frame. He plucked it up and examined it. It was part of a map. Clenching it between his fingers. "Searel. Get my horse," he commanded.

4

The Road To Deorad

"Are we almost there?" Leona's voice muffled from the inside of Dean's bag.

"No," Dean, annoyed, replied. The morning had been brutal; Dean had a pit in his stomach since the encounter in the village. Every step he took away from there was one step closer to them, putting all of this behind them.

Leona was particularly impatient when it came to traveling. She had never left the forest before, and now that she had, she was confined to a stuffy bag with Mars in the heat, and she couldn't see anything. Dean understood her frustration and was empathetic to her. However, this did little to quell the annoyance he felt every few moments when Leona would painstakingly ask if they had arrived there yet repetitively.

The trek from the village to Deorad was more daunting than the map had originally shown. They were surrounded by deep green rolling hills, roads that narrowly intersected, and nothing but stones and grass. Dean had anticipated that going this way would be the lesser of evils. He figured that by taking the path commonly used by humans, they would have less of a chance of getting lost or worse.

Leona watched the clouds dance in the sky through the flap in Dean's bag. The world was so much larger and stranger than she had ever imagined.

"The sky is endless; I had always wished we'd go on a journey; I guess I never pictured it would be as cursed fugitives, though." Leona knew that what transpired could not so easily be undone, and even with all the shame she felt, a part of her was just happy to be next to Dean and away from the inner corridors of the castle that felt like a prison.

"At least we can finally see the sea," Dean mused as the wind bellowed against him and the flap to the bag blew open. Leona poked her head all the way out, and she was in awe. Over the hills were steep cliffs and water crashing against them. They were the most beautiful shade of blue, and Leona's eyes twinkled in awe.

Even as a cat, Dean thought she was just as she was; her personality never wavered.

"Once we find Verona, and she turns me back, I want to run in grasslands and feel the sun and breeze on my face," Leona softly uttered. Dean caught a quick glimpse of the distance in her green eyes. *She's got so much riding on finding a legend from a story that was told to him as a child. What if she doesn't even exist? What if I'm completely wrong, and she stays a cat?*" Dean was anxious at the thought. He nervously tousled his hair. If Leona couldn't be turned back, what would life look like? Living life running away from humans and mages alike?

"Ugh," Dean sighed with a grimace on his face.

"You know, Dean, your attitude is a real downer," Leona crossly stated. Dean felt his eyebrow twitch with annoyance at her remark.

"My apologies, Your Highness," Dean said sarcastically. Leona, now incensed, let out a hiss.

"Even as a cat, the girl is still the very same," Mars mused with a giggle. It wasn't as if Leona wasn't grateful to Dean for doing this for her; it was her fault after all; she pushed him to basically commit treason so she could avoid the embarrassment that now seemed completely trivial in the face of this.

As the path continued winding, it seemed they had walked for an eternity. Leona was sympathetic to Dean; he seemed so tired, and she felt a twinge in her chest. Dean let out a groan and plopped himself on a small hill next to a dirt road. Leona and Mars spilled out of the bag next to him; Dean rummaged through his bag and pulled out a small pouch with dried meat and fish; he began to gnaw at it. Dean took the dried fish and broke it in half; he held one half out to Leona and the other to Mars. Mars quickly grabbed hold of it and began chewing away; Leona, however, gingerly accepted her portion; it wasn't that she didn't desire food, it was that every action felt wrong in this form, even something as natural as eating or drinking.

Leona felt like a stranger in her body.

Dean continued to gnaw at the dried meat as he kicked his feet back and stared towards the blue sky as clouds floated by. His black hair gently tousled with each breeze.

"Dean was so prince-like," Leona thought as she felt her heart beat a bit faster; perhaps she hadn't noticed it before, but the boy she knew was not the same as the one who would transverse the castle with her. Dean was strong; he was no longer a boy; in Leona's eyes, he was a man, one who looked like a prince

from another land. His piercing eyes and stark hair created a striking contrast against his sharp cheekbones.

Leona thought Dean was possibly the kindest person she knew, she often wondered what he thought of her. She was certain that he could never see her in the same light she saw him, even as royalty; she was a frail, incompetent, and according to him, *"annoying loudmouth"*; someone like Dean could never see her any other way, especially now as a cat, he certainly would never be able to unsee her this way.

She let out a disappointed sigh.

"What's up?" Dean raised one eyebrow at Leona; she felt her cheeks begin to heat as she abruptly turned around.

"Nothing," she muttered quickly.

"You're still a terrible liar, even as a cat," he countered, taking another bite.

"I–it's nothing okay" she practically hissed. Dean shifted his weight and tilted his head as he intently gazed at her, studying her as if seeking an answer she would not utter.

"You know Leona, you can tell me anything. It's not like I'll hold it against you." Dean's eyes met hers as he spoke, each word sincere.

"I was just thinking about how you don't look like a lot of the people from here..." her words were carefully chosen not to betray her thoughts.

Dean looked at her thoughtfully for a moment before leaning back again.

"I could be from somewhere else; it's not like I know anything about my parents or family." he continued to watch the clouds lazily drift by.

"Do you ever wonder where you came from?" Leona asked before she could stop herself.

"I was told I was left at the forest's edge as a baby, and thanks to your father's kindness, he allowed some of the knights to raise me, and of course, he gave me a grimoire," he paused for a moment, "I know that I was an ordinary human and I know that I was lucky to have been found. As far as anything beyond that, I have no memories or knowledge of my lineage." He softly uttered.

"I'm sorry, I didn't mean to-," he cut her off before she could finish.

"I'd answer any question for you, Leona." he smiled softly.

"Why did you choose to become a knight?" she gently asked. Dean paused, carefully considering the question before meeting her eyes again.

"I suppose it was a way for me to feel like I belonged in the forest and Caillte, that I belonged somewhere. I never quite fit, but being a knight gave me a purpose, a goal, and even a sense of belonging." his words were laced with a quiet longing.

Leona could feel herself becoming more flustered and decided to change the subject.

"How much farther is Deorad?" she asked, averting her gaze. Dean thought for a moment.

"We're probably pretty close by now." he glanced thoughtfully at the sun's position.

Mars looked between them, seemingly amused by their conversation.

"Leona, I can hear your heart beating so fast," Mars cooed playfully.

"Mars!" Leona blurted.

Dean looked between the two, unsure of what Mars had said. He gave Leona an unreadable look before shifting his gaze back to the clouds above.

41

As they traveled through the hills and dirt roads, a sign came into view: Deorad. It was crudely carved. Dean let out a sigh of relief, and they were almost there. He pulled out the makeshift map he made, and the tattered edges moved gently in the breeze. *Siren* circled beyond the mountainside just past Deorad, and there, he would be able to set things right and hopefully keep his promise to Cyrus that he swore years before.

Deorad was much like the village they left the following day, except much larger. It was loud, and the people crowding the streets were littered on every corner. Shops lined the streets along with many buildings and homes.

A woman with sharp brown eyes and locks of black ribbon-like hair danced as a man played an instrument with strings; she was not much older than them. However, her eyes were much older and tired. Dean thought she was beautiful, but in the way that stone sculptures are beautiful, this woman, for all the beauty she possessed, had none of the softness he knew from Leona.

She caught his eye and gave a sly smile, moving her hips to beckon him over. Embarrassed, Dean's cheeks began to heat, and he looked away.

The air in Deorad smelled of smoke and charred wood.

The bustle of the street was overwhelming, pushing his way through the people filled Dean with anxiety as he worried for the comfort of Leona and Mars; he had pushed through the crowds into a mostly vacant street, a tall man with raven hair and steely blue eyes was leaned against the corner of a wall, he wasn't dressed like the other people in the human realm; his clothes had a sophistication that the people around didn't have, he wore clothes not unlike the ones that seemed familiar to Caillte.

His black shirt-fitted pants and overcoat elegantly hung on his lean frame. He appeared to be from somewhere else himself. Dean had never seen someone so regal and so dangerous; even His Majesty, in all his strength, did not feel as dangerous as the man who stood before him.

He turned his eyes to meet Dean's, and he could feel the unease set in; Leona and Mars shifted anxiously in the bag. "Boy, why are you in a place like this?" His voice was cold, as he apathetically questioned Dean.

"I'm trying to get to Siren," Dean countered.

"It's unwise to travel the non-magic regions with a cursed princess and a familiar," he plainly said in passing as he began walking away from the corner he had leaned on. His coat bellowed behind him as he disappeared into the crowd.

Dean was frozen in fear. He could feel Leona and Mars stiffening through the bag's cloth.

"Who was that...?" Leona softly asked with a shaky voice; she was terrified and uneasy; something felt familiar, and perhaps there was something ethereal about him, too. He saw right through them; someone so perceptive, perhaps even dangerous, was just lurking around. Dean couldn't let Leona see how concerned he was, so he gently patted the bag.

"We need to stay away from the people of this place. There's something else going on here, and I don't want to stay around to find out." Leona agreed. Mars was oddly quiet. Leona and Dean both seemed to notice how strange she was acting. She said nothing, not a word, hiss, or meow.

The sound of commotion broke them away from their thoughts. There was screaming in the streets. Dean immediately began moving through the alleyways to try and get as far away from town as possible; he couldn't shake the feeling of cold eyes on him.

He wondered if they would see that man again, and if they did, what would he do? As they slipped out of the city limits into the tree line of the mountain pass ahead of them, Leona began to worry more intently. This was becoming more and more twisted the further they went from Caillte. Dean turned back and saw Deorad in the distance from the hills; smoke began swirling and bellowing in the sky, and the setting sun illuminating the valley in an orange glow made the scene feel almost otherworldly.

Once Dean was certain that they were not followed, he took off the bag and gently opened it, allowing the fabric to fall away completely.

Leona and Mars looked at Dean intently. Leona began stretching; Mars, however, stayed still; something was different with her; it wasn't quite right; her bright eyes seemed distant, and she hadn't uttered a word since they departed Deorad for the safety of the trees.

"Mars?" Leona asked, allowing a bit of her worry to bleed into her voice. Mars looked at Leona and gave her a reassuring look.

"I'm just tired from our journey," she mused and rubbed up against Leona; although Mars was usually lovey towards Leona, she felt like something was off.

"Is that really all?" Leona pressed gently. Mars gave a soft nudge against Leona.

"I'm quite alright," she cooed.

Leona looked at her questioningly but did not press further; she gingerly sat beside her outside the tree line. Mars seemed to relax a bit as the silence befell them. Leona noticed Dean looking particularly agitated.

"Dean?" Leona softly allowed his name to roll from her tongue.

"It isn't safe here." he looked at Leona, his blue eyes clouded with frustration and something else.

"That's why we're going to Siren," she urged

Dean looked at Leona intently as though preparing himself for her reaction.

"I think we should go back to Caillte," Dean abruptly blurted. Leona was shocked

"What!" she exclaimed.

"Leona, we need to go home. Cyrus can fix this–" Leona cut him off.

"No, he can't!" she shouted.

"How do you know?" he shouted back.

"Because!" she countered.

"Because why Leona? Because you don't want to ask him for help? Because you don't want him to know that you asked me? Or," he paused for a moment. "Because you know as well as I do that all of this was a mistake?" His anger and tension were palpable.

"How can you even say that to me? You know how he is!" she shouted back, incensed. Dean ran his fingers through his hair as he tried to keep his anger at bay.

"Well, you're cursed, and whether you like it or not, we're going home," He angrily stated.

"You can't order me around," Leona hissed. The anger welled up inside Dean, and before he could stop himself, the words escaped his lips,

"Grow up, Leona! We're not kids anymore running away from Yara and Cyrus! maybe if you royals stopped acting like you always know best, then your father wouldn't be pushing

45

the coronation on you when you can't even use magic!" Leona looked stricken hearing this from Dean. She never thought he saw her that way; she always thought he was one of the only people who saw her for who she was, aside from the title or the fact she wasn't any good at anything. She could feel her heart breaking at the realization.

"I won't go back. Not until I'm worthy..." her anger faded into defeat and then sadness.

"I just think..." Dean began, but the words failed to come. Leona's eyes investigated his, and they were filled with sadness. "I should've never allowed this..."

He didn't want to fight with her, but he also couldn't allow her to continue like this. Even if it cost Dean his head or his home or having Leona in his life at all, he'd accept responsibility so long as it meant undoing this. Dean stood up and began wandering into the trees of the forest away from Leona and Mars.

"I'm going to take a walk." He refused to meet Leona's eyes. He didn't want to see this version of him reflected in them. Before Leona could protest, he faded into the line of trees.

Leona felt tears begin to well up in her eyes.

"Leona...I think he's right," Mars softly uttered. Leona looked stricken.

"You too, huh! You think I'm just as stupid and reckless as him, don't you!" Leona spat the words at Mars.

"It isn't that-" Mars tried to defend her words.

"It is that! My entire life, I always thought you and Dean got it. I never wanted any of this!" Leona cried. You were supposed to always be on my side!" Leona's words pierced Mars, and she was taken aback.

"Leona," Mars tried to appeal to her, but Leona would not hear her; she turned away from Mars and began running towards the trees from where Dean had disappeared.

Leona ran into the line of trees; she could feel her tears streaming down her face and falling behind her as she ran into the woods; these woods reminded her of home; they were dense and thick. And had an essence of magic teeming in them. The farther she went into the woods, the more Dean's words echoed callously in her head. She knew she was reckless. She knew that everything Dean had thought of her was true; she had just hoped, believed even, that he didn't see through her.

The forest began to darken as the sun threatened to escape behind the mountainside as it set. Its soft glow was all that remained. A twinkling caught the corner of Leona's sight, and she felt her paw give way into what felt like the entrance to the heart of the kingdom, but it was different somehow. Leona felt like she hit a wall.

The force of whatever she felt knocked the wind out of her, and a soft white light surrounded her. It was all around her, so gentle and warm; soon, the light gave way to a clearing. There were trees with doors on them, almost like homes, and the chatter of children in the distance. Leona was on the ground, and she felt the draping of something soft on her skin.

Her eyes adjusted to the soft light, and she raised her head ever so slightly; a rebellious strand of crimson hair danced gently in her vision. Her green eyes were wide with tears.

Leona looked down at her hands, but they were no longer those of a beast. They were her hands. Her breath caught in her throat as her eyes looked at the inky black tendrils like vines wrapped around her pale wrist. The very same thorn-covered vines in her dream back at the Inn. Leona's confusion gave way to panic, which gave way to shock. She gathered the soft fabric that was draped on her and craned her head to see around her.

There, against a tree, was a tall man with raven hair and steely blue eyes clad in black. "Hello, Cursed Princess," he uttered mockingly with a smirk.

5

What is a Knight

As the sun began to set around them, Aver and Searel approached the beaten and winding path to Deorad, unsure of whether the one they pursued had taken refuge in the towering city. The commotion and bustle of the city were palpable. Aver was filled with rage so apparent you could see it exuding from him. Searel was as dulled-eyed as always. They rode on the backs of two of the most magnificent horses, bearing the crest of the kingdom they swore to protect.

"You probably should have waited for backup, you know," Searel stated dully; he knew Aver wouldn't have waited.

"And let some filthy mages attempt to steal the souls of our citizens. No way," Aver huffed, his golden hair tousled in and out of his eyes. He was every bit the spitting image of his father, thought Searel. The man turned his head up in a defeated annoyance.

"Yes, your Majesty, son of Aim's holy and just ruler," he

mockingly retorted.

"Shut up, Searel; I have a duty to my people," Aver spat, the anger apparent in his tone and cold stare.

"You have a duty to the throne, and if you get murdered by some half-rate mage, I'll surely be doomed along with our people." Searel was right, Aver knew as much, but he would never let that delinquent be satisfied with being correct; if they did nothing, who would do something?

The city's gates were before them, and everything was as it should be. Aver was a bit disappointed thus far; he was certain that the man he saw in the city of Tearn would be here; perhaps he was looking in the wrong places.

Searel steadied his horse with an annoyed expression and began to shout,

"By order of His Majesty, Prince Aver Althan Aims of the Kingdom of Aims, the royal knights have come in pursuit of a fugitive mage. Any information regarding the fugitive is to be brought forth immediately." The crowd began to break into a frenzy of murmurs.

Mage? What on earth? The people began to whisper among themselves. Aver had a scowl on his face. *"That imbecile had to announce his presence as if it wasn't hard enough to catch a mage. Now, the entire crowd knew they were there looking for one. Searel was a fool."* Aver thought to himself.

Searel looked pleased with himself as he had set out to ensure that Aver would not come face-to-face with that boy or any possible mage. Searel was tasked with keeping Aver safe, and this was his best way to do so.

In the crowd of whispers, a tall man clad in black with steely blue eyes smirked, and with the snap of his fingers, explosions resonated throughout the square. *BOOM!* Debris and loud crashes rang out as people began screaming and rushing; Aver's horse spooked, startled, and almost threw him off,

"After him!" he shouted. There was no way to pursue him in the ensuing chaos that was unfolding before them; the people were like a moving flood of screams, terror, and panic. Searel attempted to take charge and calm the horses while he grabbed hold of Aver,

"We must wait this out! We can't go any further until they disperse." Aver was even more furious; Searel really had a knack for getting on his last nerve, especially in situations like this. Aver was certain that the man he caught a glimpse of was not the same boy he bumped into in Tearn. They both bore a resemblance to one another, but the man he saw before the explosions rang out was older; he looked to be in his twenties, Aver thought, and although lean, appeared to be much stronger than the boy.

Something odd was happening in the Kingdom of Aims; Aver worried this was the first sign of rebellion. He thought of the stories the knights told about the war that shook the realm, *"The forest housed a race of monsters that bore the faces of humans, the mages. Like seventeen years ago, those monsters were trying to take down the kingdom."* Aver was no longer a child; he would not sit idly by and let it happen this time.

In the chaos of the crowd, he dismounted his horse, leaving Searel and his horse behind. He would not be resigned to fate, nor would he allow this chaos to continue; he sprinted towards the street where he saw that man.

Even if he couldn't find the boy, he would stomp out any embers of those who would raise a hand against the kingdom, even if it killed him.

As he rounded the corner, he happened upon a group of

citizens huddled together, covered in debris and blood. An elderly man and two young women were bleeding among the citizens. It looked as though the explosion had caught them. Aver quickly knelt beside the injured to assess the situation; the elderly man appeared to be injured worse than the two women; he was bleeding profusely and looked disoriented.

"Yyo...oour...hi...gh...ness," the man stammered between labored breaths. Aver tore at his clothes and wadded up the fabric, careful to put pressure on the wound without causing the man too much discomfort.

"It'll be okay; we will help you." He comforted the man sincerely. The man gave a weak smile and began to flutter his eyes closed; Aver felt the realization wash over him, his head down with shame. His clothes dripped in the blood of the innocent man as his breathing became shallower and slowly halted altogether.

Aver felt a firm hand on his shoulder; he turned his head, his blond hair in his eyes could not hide his tears; Searel looked at him with sympathy.

"We can save the others," he said with conviction. With that, Aver rose to his feet and began moving the debris to unpin the other citizens who had gotten caught in the explosion. Aver would give honorary partings to those who lost their lives today, usually a gesture reserved for soldiers who died in battle. He thought it was fitting since these people were innocent and nothing but casualties of a war that had been silently ripping at the seams of the kingdom for the last 100 years.

Searel and Aver continued their efforts to pull as many citizens from the rubble and debris as possible, tending to each while trying to maintain order amongst the panic and warble of the crowds. Aver felt his heartache as he saw that a few of the victims were children. He gently wiped the blood from a young boy's head as he leaned him against the wall from the ground.

"How many fingers am I holding up?" he asked the boy softly. Aver held up his gloved hand, showing two fingers. The boy looked at him with a hint of confusion before answering.

"This many," his little voice was so small as he mirrored Aver's hand. Aver gave him a kind smile as he ruffled his messy brown hair.

"You're going to be fine; I'll make sure of it," he reassured the young boy.

Searel could not help but feel a sense of pride in Aver's gentle demeanor for his people underneath his attitude and constant need to take charge. Aver was kind and fiercely loyal to his kingdom and its people.

6

A Cursed Princess

Leona was in shock and awe; she looked up at a tall man with ethereal features and intense, steely blue eyes, his long black hair cascading around him. He was striking and beautiful but also dangerous. She had never seen anyone that looked like him in Caillte before; he didn't seem human.

Leona steadied herself and made sure to keep a tight grip on the large cloth that was draped around her; her defiant green eyes pierced his.

"How do you know I'm cursed?" she asked him. His steely eyes looked directly at her wrist, where the inky vines had wrapped themselves into a crude thorn-covered bracelet. She could feel terror begin to wash over her as she took stock of the situation. She was alone, in a strange place, with a strange being that seemed to know a lot about her, and she was human again.

Leona felt her cheeks begin to heat as she realized that the cloth draped around her was the only thing covering her.

"Sivine, was it Cursed Princess?" he asked coyly.

"How do you know my middle name?" Leona was beginning to panic; this being seemed more and more dangerous with every word he uttered.

"I know lots of things...lots of people..." he turned around and began walking, beckoning her to follow. There was something so familiar about him that Leona couldn't quite place it. Leona reluctantly followed, clutching the cloth draped around her.

As they walked, Leona caught sight of others; they had the same otherworldly essence about them; they were all so strikingly beautiful, it was eerie. Leona had never heard of others outside the walls of Caillte except for the humans. She was unsure of what she was seeing, or rather walking into. The man stopped in front of a large tree embellished with lights. He opened the door and held it for her as though commanding she venture inside; she reluctantly did so, to her dismay.

She looked around; it was as though the tree itself had been hollowed out, and beautiful carvings and symbols adorned the walls; it reminded her of the palace; there were flowers everywhere, but unlike the palace, these appeared to grow from the walls themselves. It was like the forest was part of this place.

"Here," he tossed a wad of fabric at Leona; she gratefully gathered it and looked around; he pointed while turning the other way to a door. Leona walked inside and closed it behind her; it was a small room, perhaps a closet. She quickly uncrumpled the garment and saw it was a simple gown; she slipped into it and was shocked at how well it fit.

The gown was a shimmering gray. There was a small mirror in the room, and Leona thought for a second that she must look a lot like her mother; she certainly did not look like herself.

Leona left the room in a hurry, and there he was, standing in the same spot as when she left.

"Who are you?" Leona asked him earnestly.

"Names Felle and I am what you might know as a Fae, although we are often called other names, demons, elves, gods." He shifted his hair to reveal a pointed ear.

"Like in fairy tales," Leona said in disbelief with a scowl on her face.

"No child, not like the fairy tales," he said, annoyed.

"I've never heard of anyone else using magic other than the mages of Caillte," Leona questioned him.

"Who do you think taught them magic?" he asked her plainly.

"That can't be. I thought the magic came from the grimoires," Leona quietly uttered, unsure of what to believe.

"Who do you think created those?" he mused with a look of amusement on his face.

"If that's true, then why is Caillte the only magic place the humans know of?" Leona asked quizzically. Felle approached her and looked down at her; he was much taller than Leona was.

"Are you always this impetuous and single-minded?" he mocked.

"Let's say I believe you. Why am I human again?" Leona asked, annoyed at Felle's mocking tone.

"That's simple; your blood recognizes that which is of the land and trees." Felle looked bored as he said this, further confusing Leona.

"Huh?" she huffed.

"Wow, you really are rather stupid," he exclaimed, surprised, "You're half Fae," he spat the words at her.

"Mother was a mage," Leona challenged.

"Your mother was of us. As you are of us. As your magic is

of us." He corrected in a dull voice. "Your curse has no power here. You will remain as you are as long as you are among those who are of you. The barrier that separates the here from there does not allow magic that is not cast within the bounds of the veil." He stated it so simply as if Leona should have known this. Like this was just another fact.

"If I leave, I'll turn back into a cat?" Leona asked sheepishly.

"Now you're getting it; I suppose there is something in that head of yours," he laughed coldly.

"You know, I'd be more inclined to listen if you didn't keep mocking me," Leona said flatly. His fingers gently touched her wrist where the bracelet of thorns wound on her.

"This is a curse mark" Leona swallowed hard as she felt a familiarness in his touch.

"Have we met before?" she quietly uttered, careful not to meet his eyes. He removed his fingers from her delicate skin and stepped back to avoid being so close to her.

"You look like her." He changed the subject completely; Felle said it with an inclination in his voice; it surprised Leona; this was the first time his cold exterior appeared to be more than just attitude and mocking retorts.

"Who is her?" Leona's questioning eyes met his.

"Vyes," He uttered, his fingers gently pulling a strand of red between his fingers, allowing it to fall away gently.

"Did you know my mother?" Leona asked him softly.

"Yes, much like you, she was cursed," Felle said with sadness behind his eyes and a somber tone.

"My mother was cursed?" Her breath caught in her throat.

"Your false king father would hear no warnings; he would allow no help for her." Felle had anger in his tone. The words he said had a bite to them.

"My father loved my mother!" Leona spat the words right back at him. Felle locked eyes with her.

"Ownership isn't love." He looked so angry as he uttered those words.

"He didn't own her. She was the queen of Caillte!" Leona exclaimed with exasperation.

"She was a tool," Felle corrected her. Felle looked bitter; Leona wondered why he seemed to think her mother was a tool and didn't want to be in Caillte.

"Who are you to this place?" Leona asked him, a smile pulled at his lips,

"Why, I'm not a false king, and those of us are among us and remain here where the humans can't make a mess of things," Felle stated the words simply; Leona thought he was a rather confusing and irritating man.

"So, what was my mother, then?" she asked him, beckoning another answer about her lineage.

"She was of us, one of our most skilled. Truly powerful, she sought to grant the wish of a half-dead human who came to the forest. She stole a relic of the past and bound her life to his, weaving in her very soul to his. As he grew stronger, she weakened, slowly draining her of all her magic and then her life force. She committed an ultimate taboo of the very magic that granted her the power to do so, in turn cursing herself, much like you did when you decided to try and claim power that was not yours to claim." Felle began to walk away.

"You can't just say that and then leave," Leona huffed.

"Can't I?" Felle turned around and once again approached Leona; getting mere inches from her face, he looked directly at her, "Cursed Princess, you are welcome to stay. But I grow bored of rehashing a history long since passed." Felle said these words sincerely, and the distance between them made Leona uncomfortable. She didn't even like Dean being this close to her.

"I have to find Dean and Mars-" Leona started before Felle cut her off.

"The human who deserted you, and the familiar? They can't enter these sacred lands. The barrier won't allow them to." he stated this, so as a matter of fact, it irritated Leona to her core.

"How did you know he left?" Leona was suspicious of Felle. He gave her a piercing glance.

"How indeed." He plainly stated.

"Then I'm leaving," she stated defiantly. Felle looked annoyed. "Then you will turn back into your cursed form, and I will bring you back," he challenged.

"You can't do that!" Leona shouted.

"I may have failed to keep my people from death before, but I've learned. I won't make that mistake again." He turned around, straightened himself, and walked down the long corridor, fading from Leona's view.

"What a jerk," she muttered under her breath. And what did he mean about keeping people from death? Why is he so cryptic and confusing?

"Miss," a lyrical-like voice echoed into the room. A small girl with vibrant orange hair and pink eyes wearing shimmering gowns that looked to hold every color of the rainbow approached her. "Who are you?" Leona asked the strange girl. The girl appeared to be no older than Leona; come to think of it, Felle didn't seem that much older than her.

"I am Ileya; I will show you to a place you may rest," she beamed. What a weird place. Leona put her head in her hands; she was an idiot. And now Mars and Dean are out there, and she's stuck with possibly one of the most confusing and irritating people she's met so far, but at least she's not a cat right now.

The girl led her down the same corridor that Felle had disappeared into. It opened into a great hall with winding staircases on either side, adorned with twisted branches and vines.

It was beautiful there.

The sound of a waterfall in the distance caught her attention as she followed along the winding stairs leading to an even larger area that overlooked the forest. There, off in the distance, was a waterfall. The forest was even more beautiful than Caillte; the wind bellowed around her, and the sun shone in soft rays.

"Here, miss," the soft voice said, gesturing to a door off the main hall. It overlooked the ledge that she was so taken with. The room was softly lit, with flowers and vines everywhere and a bed larger than the one she knew.

"I need to leave-" She stammered; Ileya raised her small hand to silence her,

"You cannot, I'm afraid; you would revert back to your cursed form, and the life would continue to be sapped out of you. King Felle would never allow someone to die a cruel death such as that." Her words shocked Leona to her core.

"King!?" Leona was stunned.

"Yes, Miss, he is our king and protects the lands here and the rest of us," Ileya said softly. She was quite possibly the most elegant and delicate being Leona had ever seen.

"Be not afraid; you will have peace here," she beamed, closing the door behind her. Leona's mind was frantic; this was all too much. She was to ascend the throne; *how many days had it been?* She anxiously thought. She had been gone for three, or was it four days? Mars is all alone. Dean is gone. She hadn't thought she was here that long, yet the sun began to soften as dusk approached.

Leona felt tears prick her eyes as they began to roll down her cheeks. If everything Felle said was true, then why had Father never uttered a single word about her? Leona was always told that her mother was a powerful mage who rivaled even the royal bloodlines of Caillte, and yet Felle called her a tool for them. If the Fae wrote the grimoires, then why were there so many at the heart of the kingdom? Leona was terrified, and beyond that, she was angry. She felt as though she had been lied to her entire life. She was tired of being treated as some fragile child waiting to be molded into the perfect heir. Cat or not, curse or not. She was going to Siren, and she would set things straight.

After she got Verona to break her curse, she would confront her father and hear the words from his lips.

She wiped the tears that had soaked her face and straightened herself; she was going to leave her destiny to herself; she would stand on her own.

Leona began searching the room to find whatever she could use to escape this place; she looked underneath the lavish bed with more blankets and pillows than even those in the Castle at home; in the corner was a small door; Leona twisted the knob and it opened onto a balcony that overlooked the waters below, a mirror of the back side of the waterfall she had just seen. The sun had given way to darkness, and she gasped. The night sky entranced Leona's eyes; there were more stars than she had ever seen in her life. She had never seen a sky like this, even in her wildest dreams. The wind blew her hair around her gently, and Leona felt a slight chill prick her skin.

In a few short strides, she had crossed the room to the door, which she entered. After a deep breath, Leona swung the door open and charged out, crashing into what felt like a wall. Leona closed her eyes and instinctively braced for the fall, but it never came. She felt a warm hand holding her up, one on her slender waist and the other on her arm. She opened her eyes to see annoyed blue ones staring back.

"What are you doing?" Felle asked her crossly.

"I must get out of here. I can't leave them out there alone!" Leona shouted at him and ripped her arm away from his.

"Even though he left you behind, leaving you to die?" His voice filled with contempt, "Yes." Leona uttered,

"You're a fool. Just like your mother." He spat the words at her.

"How am I supposed to believe a word you say when you only speak in riddles and nonsense!" Leona was furious. Felle's eyes met hers; they looked wild, as if emotion had consumed him.

He grabbed her hand and pulled her to the ledge overlooking the waterfall in the distance. The sun had given way to night, and the silver-streaked sky full of stars welcomed the pale rays of the moonlight.

"Very well, Cursed Princess." Fury plain in his eyes, "A century ago, when we were still fledglings younger than you are now, the humans approached our tribe; they said they wanted to understand. My father was the keeper of The Isles then, and he believed them. The Fae created the grimoires. This was to be a token of the beginnings of an understanding. Peace between the realms. The humans took the magic they found within and used it to wage wars against each other.

My father was slain in that war among many of our folk. By the time I had taken up his mantle, we had been driven to the depths of extinction. I sealed the barrier to prevent mortal hands from playing in the blood of our people any longer. Our people were taken, slain, sacrificed for the humans to continue to slaughter each other, and we were mere collateral damage.

Vyes saw so much senseless bloodshed the wars caused; even her younger brother was slain. 20 years ago, while she traversed the forbidden woods outside the barrier, she happened across a human that was mortally wounded, another person caught in the crossfire.

She took pity on that human and asked him if he wanted to live. That human lied to her and fed her a promise of a nonexistent world. She believed him and stole an ancient relic from the inner walls of the spirit tree that resides in the innermost part of The Isles. She used that relic to weave their destinies and, in turn, cursed herself. Every breath became shared, the blood that pumped through her veins bid to him and him alone; her very essence and life force became the embers that kept his dying life force going.

After it had been done, the humans spirited her away to their realm without so much as a word. I thought she was dead... another casualty of war between the humans...it took me 3 years to find her." Felle's eyes met hers; the anger had faded and was replaced by a deep sadness.

"When I did, I confronted the human she cursed herself for; I begged him to allow her to return so that I could stop her curse. He refused, and she would not defy him. I remember seeing her again after all that time. Her hair was just as crimson as in The Isles when the sun used to dance its golden rays off it.

She was exactly as she was, except her belly was swollen with a child. She was so beautiful. You would have never known the curse that had almost completely consumed her if it weren't for the curse marks that bound her on her ankles, wrists, and neck.

Like a twisted shackle for an animal." Leona felt tears burn her eyes once again as she felt the weight of this long-hidden truth fall upon her.

"It can't be true...how could it be possible when you are a man of no older than 25?" Her voice was barely a whisper as the tears began to fall.

"No lies have parted my lips. I'm sure your father would rather die himself than admit the shameful truth of his actions. He wanted to possess her even if it was as a corpse. As far as my age, we Fae do not experience the same half-life that humans do. The sands of time drop ever slower than that of humans. They are such fragile, fleeting creatures. They continue to destroy even with the knowledge of their ever-swift existence." Felle's words were dripping with contempt.

"I never intended to burden you with this." His voice softened as he reached his slender hand to her face and wiped the falling tears.

"Why didn't he save her...?" Leona uttered through tears.

"I do not have the answer you seek...Based on the human's actions, I can only imagine that it was to obtain power. Vyes was many things, and her power rivaled that of my own." Felle's voice was filled with sadness.

"Why does no one know of the wars...?" Leona questioned weakly. "17 years ago, they ended. An armistice was formed between the human kingdoms of Aims and Caillte. The humans forbade magic outside of the lost forest, and in turn, the lost forest forbade humans inside its grounds." Felle leaned against the railing of the balcony and looked onward. "It's all been lies," Leona uttered. Betrayal was evident in her voice. "The humans only lie." Felle spat the words as if they were dirty. "Not all of them," Leona meekly corrected.

"Do you still wish to continue this senseless endeavor?" Felle's words were dripping with conviction as he gazed at her. Leona took a long moment before meeting his eyes back.

"Even if it is all lies. Even if my father is this monster. Even if I regret it, I won't abandon them." Leona's voice did not waver, even though every word felt as though it was tearing her apart. She knew deep within herself that there were many things about Caillte and the Kingdom of Aims that defied answers, even so, she refused to believe that every word Felle had said could be accurate. Perhaps he was led astray, or perhaps she was in denial. Either way, Leona would not allow herself to be convinced yet. Felle's eyes softened, and he approached her.

"You're being foolish. If you leave this place, the curse you put on yourself will kill you by the light on the next full moon." Felle uttered the words softly; they were filled with sadness. He looked into Leona's tear-stained eyes.

"Fool or not, I won't abandon them..." she uttered, shifting her gaze. Felle let out a sigh and softened; he looked irritated but didn't seem angry.

"If you go, I can't promise I'll be able to help you undo what you've done; the boy and the familiar will not be able to undo it either." Felle looked sincere as he said these words.

"Even if I die, I'd rather do it on my terms, even if it's the only thing I've ever been able to choose for myself." Leona could not believe she had admitted that to this stranger. Felle looked somber; he lifted his hand to push back the rebellious strand of hair that had fallen over Leona's eye. He lingered there momentarily; Leona could feel the heat returning to her cheeks.

"Very well. We will depart." He said matter of fact.

"We?" Leona asked him.

"You are resigned to dying, and I told you already that I will not allow any more of my people to die," he countered.

"You can't come with me; I-" Leona couldn't finish her sentence before Felle began pulling her alongside him toward the spiraling stairs.

"If I don't go with you, you will likely escape anyway and end up dying among the humans; you have not yet awoken Sivine." He trailed off as if lost in thought.

"My name is Leona," she exclaimed.

"Your true name is Sivine." He countered.

"My name is Leona," she corrected him again as they continued down the spiraling stairs and out into the winding corridors. Leona looked at his hand on hers, pulling her along, and was deeply confused; why would he do this? He was so against me leaving a moment ago. He is genuinely so irritating.

Felle pulled Leona with him toward a different door down the last corridor. It had vines enveloping it, reminding Leona of the vines on the grimoire. Her curse mark looked like a twisted and mutilated form of these very vines. Felle touched the door, and the vines unattached themselves and retreated into the walls, allowing the door to open to a room full of the most books Leona had ever seen. The books lined every section of the walls, and the floors had stacks upon stacks of tomes.

"I've never seen so many books," she breathed in awe. He immediately began sifting through the piles of books that lined the room, throwing them behind him and creating clouds of dust as he continued searching. *Cough, cough*, Leona began to cough from the cloud of dust encompassing the room. Felle kept intently sifting through books; he moved quickly as if laser-focused on a singular thought.

"Ah, there it is," he uttered to himself. A book that looked eerily like that of the one that Leona had when she cursed herself. Felle opened the pages, but the light did not erupt from it; instead, a small necklace came out; it had the most delicate crystal flowers encasing a vial. Felle opened the vial and, in one swift motion, sliced his finger with a small blade he pulled from his pocket and allowed the vial to fill with blood.

"What are you doing!" Leona demanded in shock. Felle threw the book behind him into the pile of discarded tomes.

"This is of the forest and us. I don't know if it will keep you human beyond the veil, but it is worth a try." Felle offered the necklace to her with an extending hand, his blood running down the chain and dripping from where he sliced his finger.

"You didn't have to hurt yourself-" Leona couldn't finish her sentence as Felle moved quickly behind her and fastened the necklace around her neck. She felt awful that this stranger was willing to go so far to help her when she was merely a nuisance to him.

"Let's go find the deserter and the familiar," Felle stated resigned to the situation. She followed him out of the room, and the moment the door shut behind them, the vines that had retreated began to crawl back over the door, effectively sealing it. Leona had so many questions, and Felle seemed to only say things that gave her more questions. She hurried behind him as he continued through the clearing to the area Leona fell through.

"Ladies first," he sarcastically said as he pushed Leona through the barrier. She was taken aback as she stumbled back into the forest, promptly hitting the ground behind her. Her eyes clenched shut.

"Still human," he mused; he looked at her with curiosity.

Leona was excited and annoyed as she looked at her arms, they were her arms. No fur and no cat features, she could tell. The curse mark glaring against her pale skin also remained. Felle was so irritating and strange. Leona didn't understand why he was even helping her.

"What was the place we left called? I never got to ask..." Leona asked him,

"The Isles," Felle stated flatly, offering Leona his hand. She took it, and he pulled her from the ground.

"How pretty," Leona softly muttered to herself.

She looked around the forest and tried to remember from which direction she had run away from Mars earlier. The sun had retreated and gave way to night; the stars dimly illuminated the sky. She had to find Mars quickly and then Dean. Dean. What was she even going to say to Dean, *"Hey Dean, that scary guy we met in Deorad is coming with us, and oh yeah, he gave me a creepy necklace filled with blood to keep me human; by the way, he isn't a human, and apparently, I'm also not completely one either. By the way, I'm going to die if I don't break my curse,"* Leona thought to herself, and a look of painful irritation crossed her face as she imagined how she could explain this. Did she even want to see Dean? Would he even want to see her?

7

Destiny is A Fickle Thing

Dean was frantically pacing; he had returned not long after Leona had left. Mars was a nervous wreck, tears in a steady stream rolled down her small cheeks. Dean was so angry at himself; how could he act so coldly to her? He knew Leona wasn't like the others in Cailtte, she was never cruel or judgmental. He regretted every word he had said to her that was dripping with anger.

Leona must've been just as terrified as he was, Dean knew deep down that he wasn't angry at Leona, more so that he was angry at himself. He should've never taken her to the grimoires, and it's not like Leona has any control over what Cyrus decides for her. Dean hung his head in his hands, his black hair a tussled mess. Mars nuzzled him. "We're both idiots," he said to Mars.

"You are." Leona's voice came from behind them; Dean snapped to attention and turned around so quickly he almost fell over; Leona was human. Her long crimson locks flowed wildly around her, and her pale skin almost shimmered in the

69

soft light cascading between the trees. She wore a simple gown reminiscent of clothing in Caillte, and around her neck hung a small necklace with a floral design and some kind of liquid swirling ever so slightly inside. On her wrist was a stark black mark resembling a rose's twisted vines.

Leona didn't look like the same person before she opened the grimoire; something was different. Dean could not quite place it. Mars and Dean were both in utter shock and disbelief.

To even more of Mars and Dean's dismay, a tall, lean man clad in black stood behind Leona. She didn't appear surprised at all. "Get away from her!" Dean shouted at the man. Felle smirked and looked at him cocking his head to the side,

"Hello, deserter, name's Felle," he mused arrogantly.

"Stop it, Dean! Felle is the reason I'm even human right now," she exclaimed.

"No way. No way, absolutely no way! Leona, what are you even saying? Stop being reckless!" Dean reached for her hand to pull her away from the tall, strange man, and just as quickly, Felle smacked his hand away.

"You seem awfully entitled for a deserter," Felle spat at Dean. Dean could feel his face getting red from embarrassment. "What happened, Leona?" Dean's eyes pleaded, searching for answers, some explanation as to why she was human and who this was.

"I'm still cursed..." she paused for a moment, "this is my curse mark." She lifted her arm to reveal the intricate and crude vines that encased her wrist in black. "Felle gave me this to keep me from changing back." Her fingers lightly trailed over the necklace that hung gently on her neck.

"If he has that power, then he can break your-" Dean was unable to finish as Felle's smooth voice uttered, "I cannot break a curse I did not cast," Felle's demeanor was somber and a bit of something else, condescending almost.

"Then what good are you?" Dean retorted with annoyance. "More good than you," Felle stated, pushing the tip of his long index finger into Dean's chest.

"We need to go to Siren," Leona cut in, trying to redirect the conversation. Felle looked annoyed but said nothing; he merely watched through cold, steely eyes.

"Leona, how can we go to Siren with this stranger? We don't know anything about him, and we also don't even know if Verona is there. He just said he can't break your curse, so he doesn't need to come," Dean continued, his voice raising with every word.

"Felle is coming." Leona huffed at Dean. Leona was surprised; she felt anger and hurt boil up inside her at Dean's assertion that she was being reckless or didn't know what she was doing. *"You don't get it,"* Leona thought to herself; she didn't want to waste time arguing with Dean or explaining what Felle had told her in The Isles. Dean would probably insist they just go home and have Cyrus handle everything. However, Leona would not return like this; there was too much she did not know, and Felle seemed to have some inclination of what those answers may be; if Leona was careful, clever even, she might be able to understand the burning questions that were consuming her very being.

Mars didn't know what to say or think. She knew exactly who was standing near Leona, and it terrified her. Leona could no longer hear Mars as a human; she couldn't even talk to her at this point. Dean was so angry he thought his head might explode.

Leona began stomping off toward Deorad; *"she was so stub-*

born," Dean thought as he slung the bag over his shoulder and gathered Mars. Felle, closely in tow behind Leona, made it a point to turn ever so slightly and flash a wicked smile at Dean every so often.

"I hate that guy." Dean groaned while carrying Mars in his arms, walking behind them. How could this have gotten so messed up? Leona was barely speaking to him, and Mars was back to Leona, not understanding a single musing from her. And now they're being accompanied by a tall, eerie being that doesn't feel human. Leona hangs onto his every word, heading towards Siren to track down a legend. Dean was scowling as his thoughts continued.

Felle seemed to be amused by being a thorn in Dean's side. He was angry at himself for leaving after they argued. He shouldn't have gone; if he hadn't, then perhaps Leona wouldn't be listening to this thing. No one even bothered to explain how suddenly she was human again or how long it would last; Leona only insisted on proceeding further. Dean hated being in the dark about things; nothing irritated him more.

The trek to Siren seemed to last an eternity. The night sky was a deep indigo above. "I think it's best we stop for a while until the sun's up," Dean offered his thoughts.

"Afraid of the dark?" Felle teased coyly. "It's not safe to be walking in the dark like this; someone could see us." Dean bitterly replied. Dean was even more annoyed now. Leona said nothing, and they continued walking. The road was dark, and the trees didn't help the light of the moon shine on the path. With a flick of Felle's wrist, a flame appeared, illuminating the road.

"Wow! That's incredible!" Leona exclaimed. She was in awe of Felle's ability to use magic with something as simple as a snap of his fingers.

"Show off," Dean uttered, each word dripping with contempt. *Snap* a flame illuminated near Dean and Mars. "I can use magic," Dean stated dryly.

"That's rather ungrateful deserter," Felle mused. With another flick of his wrist, the flame dispersed when he snapped his fingers.

"My name is not deserter!" Dean huffed. Glaring intently at Felle. *Snap, the flame ignited once again,* to Dean's dismay.

"Here, boy". Felle teased, a wicked smirk tugging at his lips once again.

"Felle?" Leona's voice warned. She appeared annoyed.

"What is it, Cursed Princess?" Felle asked innocently.

"Don't call me Cursed Princess," Leona retorted, irritation plain on her face.

"Are we almost to Siren?" Leona asked him. He pointed towards a thick line of trees.

"Past those are the cliffs that overlook Siren," he replied emotionless. Leona thought Felle was rather strange. He seemed like a completely different person than the one that spoke to her in The Isles; he was snarky and cold, not the slightly less cold, almost gentler version he was when they were alone. *"Why should I even care?"* Leona tried to shake the thoughts from her head.

The line of trees before them was beginning to wane as they overlooked the cliffside. The sound of crashing waves was evident, the night sky was clear, and the moon's light illuminated the ripples on the tides far below.

Leona had never seen an ocean before, much less one at night. The salty sea air and the torrent breeze were new to her. The cliffside looked over the ocean, and the ocean town nestled below; soft light glowed from the small shops and homes. "This must be Siren," Leona breathed. They finally made it; all that was left was to find Verona, and then she could break Leona's curse; finally, Leona could go home and face her father. Only then could she finally confront the past and all the ghosts and secrets attached to it.

As they made their way down the cliffside, careful not to draw attention to themselves or fall, Felle's flames followed them, gently illuminating the path before them. He strode down the hillside nonchalantly; he never once looked down.

His silhouette in the moonlight looked like something from a fairy tale. His tall, lean frame moved effortlessly. He was elusive, mysterious, and dangerous; he reminded Leona of a Tiger. He was elegant and even beautiful but unpredictable. She thought that Felle almost looked like Dean in a certain way. Dean's discontent was evident. Even Leona caught a glimpse of it as he followed her gaze to Felle.

"What?" Leona blurted out as she blushed from embarrassment. She did not want Dean to utter anything about Felle, Siren, or any other protests or grievances. He infuriated her, and she still imagined the bitter words he spat at her before she found herself in *The Isles*.

"Leona," Dean began but stopped himself. He seemed like he wanted to say more, but the words would not come out. *"Of course, the moment it counts, a word won't escape my lips,"* he thought to himself. He was embarrassed, frustrated, exhausted, and more than anything, he didn't want Felle around Leona at all.

The soft illumination of the town drew them in as they moved through the brush between the mountainside cliffs onto the cobblestone streets that lined this coastal town. A tavern off the path was illuminated the brightest, it was an old stone building with driftwood hanging from it like archaic ornaments. The door, an old board with a crudely carved name, *The Sirens Nest*, they had finally made it. They were in Siren.

8

The Sirens Nest

The tavern was crowded with people loudly clanking their cups, the sound of weathered wood being sloshed with liquid, and a loud piano playing echoed throughout the building. The tavern was well-lit, and the bitter smell of ale was present in the air. Felle had no reservations, nor did he bear an ounce of humble behavior toward anyone as he allowed his shoulder to push into the people around him at the tavern, effectively knocking them aside as he casually brushed past. Leona, Dean, and Mars followed behind and saw the disgust on the other humans' faces at this bold show of carelessness from Felle.

Dean looked as though he was brooding; the muscle in his jaw would twitch ever so often when he looked in the general direction of Felle. Leona knew that look well. Since they were children, Dean would clench his teeth like that whenever he was angry, and from the looks of it, he was slightly furious at Felle's existence. Leona could feel her face pull into a scowl. She thought Dean's head would burst into flames from all his pent-up anger at the Fae, who was entirely filled with himself.

He approached the bar in a few long strides; a woman who looked to be in her thirties was at the counter; her long silver hair was pulled back in braids that formed like a crown around her head, she had silver eyes and lightly freckled skin, she wasn't a very tall woman, she was barely taller than Leona, unlike Leona though, this woman although slender bore the figure of a woman and not a girl. Leona thought she was truly lovely. "I'm looking for someone," Felle asserted to the woman.

"Someone huh? Lots of someone's around here." She leaned against the ledge of the bar and took a large swig of the frothy liquid in her mug before slamming it down; the frothy liquid swished out of the cup and swirled around the top of the bar.

As Leona took a closer look at the woman, she noticed her face was flushed. She let out a hearty laugh right into Felle's perturbed face. Felle brought his slender fingers to the bridge of his nose and made a gesture as though he could feel a headache coming on. Pure annoyance was painted across his usually emotionless face.

"Verona is her name," Leona said softly to the woman before Felle had a chance to lash her with his sharp tongue and possibly ruin any chance of gaining information. The woman looked Leona up and down, a questioning look on her face; she put her hand to her hip and wagged her finger at Leona's face.

"No one here by that name, kid. It's best to go home." She gave Leona a serious look. Leona's face fell,

"Do you know where I can find her?" Leona asked,

"No one in Siren with that name, kid," the woman retorted before grabbing the mug on the bar and taking another heavy swig of liquid.

"A drunk barkeep, how inconvenient' Felle remarked, annoyance clear in his tone.

"Drunk?" Dean asked, confused. Felle gave him an emotionless glance.

"You don't know a lot, do you, boy?" Felle asked flatly.

"I know lots of things!" Dean asserted back. Felle's blue eyes pierced his, a wicked smile pulling at his lips, "You don't even know the Cursed Princesses' true name" he uttered mockingly.

"Leona is her name," Dean spat back, feeling anger grow in him.

"Is it?" Felle said teasingly. He leaned back against the bar, shutting his eyes and tilting his head towards the ceiling, effectively ignoring Dean and any retort he could muster. Dean was even more furious at the attitude this stranger dared to have. Dean looked around, and Leona was nowhere to be seen; he lost sight of her when he began arguing with Felle.

Leona was crushed; she could not bear the acrid smell of ale, nor could she stomach the noise any longer, and swiftly slipped through the door to the outside of the tavern.

The night sky had not yet given way to the sunrise, but the stars seemed to twinkle less. *"If there was truly no Verona here, then I have no chance of breaking my curse. I can never go home."* It was a solemn thought to have, and Leona knew all too well that the necklace Felle had given her was likely temporary; she had noticed the blood swirling in it had begun to diminish since they left *The Isles*.

Not even a full day had passed, and she had a strong suspicion that as time went on, it would grow less effective, and her cursed form would return. Felle's words echoed in her mind.

She would die by the next full moon if she stayed out of The Isles and its barrier.

Leona turned to the night sky above; the moon was not quite full. However, it couldn't be more than a week away before it was. Dean would surely make her return to Cailtte now. No Verona, no cure. And without a cure, it was either death by her curse, or her father may well execute Dean and still not be able to undo this. Leona could feel the despair as it enveloped her; she slunk back against a rock near the tavern, her plans in ruins. Tears began to stream down her face as reality set in.

"Why're you looking for Verona anyway?" a woman's voice asked softly behind Leona; she turned her head and realized the familiar voice belonged to the woman at the bar.

"I know she's a mage, and I came to seek her help," Leona mustered through tears. She tried to swipe away before they could be noticed. "What kind of help could a mage give a kid like yourself?" the woman leaned down and gave a sincere look. "I need her help breaking a curse," Leona muttered, barely a whisper, as she lifted her wrist, revealing the curse mark.

"Curse, you say?" She touched her finger to her mouth as her eyes looked onto the curse mark; she then turned her attention towards her forehead as if thinking intently; a sad look crossed her carefree face, and her eyes met Leona. "I'm sorry, kid, I can't break those," she said gently. Leona was shocked as she realized that this woman standing in front of her must be the mage they were seeking. "you're Verona the Veracious?" Leona frantically asked. Leona's eyes were wide with hope.

"I don't go by that name anymore, kid." She corrected Leona pointedly. "My name's Leona, and I tried to use a grimoire that I stole from the Kingdom of Cailtte, and it exploded, and I turned into a cat, and I-" Leona frantically allowed the words to stumble out of her mouth in a frenzy. The woman cut her off with a look of utter shock as her mouth stood agape.

"Cyrus's kid?" she asked in utter disbelief. "You know my dad!?" Leona exclaimed. The woman gave an annoyed look, "yeah, I know him, and he's probably throwing himself a good little fit that his daughter is missing and cursed," she muttered, shifting her gaze.

"Then it's true! You are the mage, and you can help me!" Leona's tone filled with hope once again as she spoke. "I can't," the woman sternly said. "But I-" Leona stammered. "Listen, kid, I can't break curses; no one can, and that little thing you've got there," The woman pointed to the necklace around her neck. "Isn't gonna fix it either. The only person who can break a curse is the same one who created it. You gotta break your own curse," She looked at Leona intently; Leona was confused; she couldn't even use magic to any applicable standard, let alone be skilled enough to break a curse.

"I can't use magic," Leona softly said. "You did when you cursed yourself." The woman replied. "No, the grimoire did," Leona corrected. "Grimoires are pure magic; they aren't capable of cursing humans; you just didn't know how to wield it and created the curse. If you can create the curse, you can break it," The woman spoke with sincerity.

"I don't know how..." Leona whispered as tears began to fall from her emerald eyes once again. "Guess you'll have to figure it out," The woman offered her hand to Leona; she took it gingerly and pulled her to her feet.

The breeze blew Leona's hair. "If you're not Verona, then who are you?" Leona asked shyly.

"The people here know me as Adira," she said with a soft smile. "Adira, will you teach me how?" Leona sheepishly

80

inquired. Adira let out a hearty laugh and smacked the back of Leona's shoulder, almost knocking her over,

"You're very persistent for a Princess, you know that," she chuckled.

"So, you won't help me?" Leona's voice fell.

"I never said that," Her face softened. "I have no intention of leaving you to be eaten up by your curse," Her words reinvigorated Leona's hope.

Leona could feel exhaustion begin to set in with each breath, her breathing slightly heavier than a moment before. "You can't learn half asleep," Adira pulled Leona alongside her back through the tavern doors and around the bar's counter.

Completely ignoring the patrons and their lingering gazes. Felle and Dean stared after in confusion as to why this woman was leading Leona away and immediately began to follow. Adira had led them to the back of the tavern, which exposed a small doorway that led into a cottage-like area; the walls were littered with parchments of pressed flowers.

Leona's eyes caught sight of the most beautiful bird she had ever seen in the most intricate birdcage she had ever encountered. The twisted gold wire along each twisted stem of the cage was delicately crafted to resemble flowers. The vibrant feathers of the bluebird inside cast a lively contrast.

Beyond the cage was a small kitchen and hall. Adira led them down the hall from the intricately crafted cage to where two carved wood doors met. Adira opened the first, revealing a small bedroom. The bed was large for the room's size, with fluffy blankets and a mountain of pillows. The walls, a dull white, were adorned with more parchment ingrained with pressed flowers.

A small window off the side revealed the tiniest hint of dusk;

Adira quickly closed the curtains to block out the first light of Daybreak. "You can sleep in here," Leona was grateful. She threw herself on the bed, and it felt as though it was made of a thousand cool feathers. The bed creaked as she felt the weight of another next to her; she turned to see Mars' eyes reflecting.

Leona had barely seen Mars since they left the trees beyond Deorad. Her small frame pushed up against Leona as if signaling that things were okay between them. Felle's eyes shifted to the black ball of fur, and a hint of something crossed his face; just as quickly as it was there, it was gone; he was back to his apathetic and rather emotionless form. He was not quick enough to completely hide that inclination from the eyes of Dean, who watched him intently as though he was a fox preparing to devour a hen.

Adira opened the other door across the hall; it, too, gave way to a bedroom, though one smaller and less inviting than the one Leona had laid claim to. "You can have this one," Adira turned her heel and began venturing back to the Tavern,

"I am not sharing a bed with that thing," Dean's words dripped with anger and contempt.

"Fine by me, sleep outside, boy," Felle mockingly retorted.

"*Tsk tsk tsk.*" Adira's glare seemed to pierce through walls. Dean's face was contorted into a grimace and a scowl. "I don't much care for the likes of either of you; if you impend my work, I will curse you far more severely than that idiot managed to curse herself. Are we clear?" Adira was rather menacing.

"I'm not sharing a bed with a human, but," Felle met her piercing eyes, "do what you must," his head cocked to the side, allowing his hair to fall away ever so slightly, exposing his pointed ear; Felle's words, were another act of defiance, rather a more subtle one than usual.

Adira's silver eyes filled with anger and shock as she saw the point of his ear. She tightly clenched her fist next to her side and continued back to the tavern without another word. Felle leaned against the frame of the door that Dean stood next to. He looked down on him and met his gaze intensely. "Perhaps, I'll sleep in her room," Felle uttered coyly as a smirk began tugging at his lips. Dean's face revealed a twitch. He shifted his gaze.

Felle sensed Dean's discomfort; he leaned against the door, quickly glancing at Leona's slumped form on the bed, "She certainly shows a lot of skin for a princess, don't you think?" Felle coyly asserted. Dean angrily closed the door to Leona's room and faced the smug man.

"Just because Leona seems to think you aren't an entirely creepy freak doesn't mean I'll allow you to mess with her," Dean glared with a cold fury at Felle's smirk.

"I see, so you would rather sleep in her room, boy?" Felle teased, causing Dean's face to turn a bright shade of red. He let out a cold laugh as he pushed from the wall and into the unoccupied room, shutting the door behind him. Dean was left standing in the hall, angry at himself for allowing Felle another opportunity to mess with him.

9

Bloodlines

The sun cascaded on Aver's head, illuminating his golden hair; he sat against a tall stone wall, the clinking of his armor softly rattled as he sunk his head back.

The ceilings of the castle were vast. Aver's eyes pierced the metal-sheathed hand in front of him; although they gleamed silver, he could not stop picturing blood running down them. He couldn't stop replaying the scene he saw the day before in Deorad. All the innocent people that faced devastation at the hands of the mages. He slammed his clenched fist into the stone of the wall behind him.

"What good will pouting do?" Searel's steely eyes and stoic expression were a welcome distraction from Aver's thoughts.

"Shut up," Aver's golden eyes narrowed into a glare. Searel held out his hand to Aver as he met his gaze,

"The king would like to see you now," Searel said sincerely to Aver as he nodded toward the large hallway. They walked mostly in silence, the only sound being the clinking of metal against stone as they continued through the castle.

The castle was magnificent, as was to be expected of the Kingdom of Aims, the never-ending halls that gave way to great rooms and beautiful balconies. These intricately crafted and grand shows of power were but one facet of the pride of the kingdom that Aver so loved and fought to improve. That was the very reason he became a royal knight; how could he expect to be king if he could not understand the plight of his people? Aver composed himself as they turned the corner to reveal two large, daunting doors of rosewood and metal embellishments.

The throne room was as intimidating as it was magnificent, with tapestries, stone statues, and servants scattered throughout.

"Announcing his Great and Just Majesty King Cassian Cross Aims the 32nd." A large throne adorned with gold and white marble housed a man no older than his forties; his golden hair fell carelessly around him, and a large and impressive crown sat above it, barely a different shade of gold than that of his hair. The crown was encrusted with jewels of every color you could imagine. His violet eyes were kind, and his regal face was that of the stories; he was adorned in a white robe with a robust feather collar and gold detailing.

To his side, the king's guard flanked him. A tall man with raven hair and slate-colored eyes stood to the right of his throne, and off to the side, he appeared to be in his forties.

He condescendingly tilted his head to the side, "Take a knee, or I'll take your head," His tone was threatening.

"It's quite alright, Rowan," he waved his elegant hand. "Aver, dear boy, tell me of Deorad," His voice was smooth, almost lyrical. The king's kind and regal demeanor was evident in the sincerity of his words.

Searel and Aver took a knee before the throne, bowing their heads in a show of respect as they recounted the events. Aver could feel the embarrassment and shame begin to rise to the surface as he explained the situation that was befalling the kingdom.

"Where is this mage now?" the king asked, concern evident in his voice.

"I...don't know," Aver could feel the ever-mounting pressure as the silence grew louder and, with it, his shame.

The king took a moment to consider. After what felt endless to Aver, he finally spoke "Rowan," as if giving a command. The king's guard immediately responded, "Inform Mercer and Auden that they are to accompany you to Deorad to hunt the mage," Searel's tired face fell as his stoic expression cracked under the weight of the command. "What about me, Father!" Aver interrupted.

"You are the Crown Prince," The kind and mild-mannered demeanor of the king was gone in an instant, "You are not to interact with the mage," his words were not a warning but rather a command. "Father I-" His violet eyes piercing as he rose from his throne and approached Aver who was still knelt in front of him, his fingers tilted Aver's chin upwards to force him to meet his eyes. "I am the king. My word is law. Return to your chambers and lick the wounds of your pride. Depart from my sight and do not return until you have accepted responsibility for the failures at your feet. You are not a child anymore, Aver," He pulled his hand away; his demeanor towards Aver was stern, and his words were sharp. However, his eyes held a softness even as he spoke them.

The servants followed behind him as he departed the throne room, the large doors closing behind him. Aver felt as though he would implode. Searel stood up silently beside him and began walking to the door. Reluctantly, Aver followed suit.

"I suppose I'll be cleaning up your mess, dear Brother," a mocking voice echoed down the hall; there stood Rowan, along with two white-haired knights, one with long flowing white hair and a strong angular face who looked to be in his thirties, the other a white short haired knight with a thin face and sharp features, not unlike the first, he appeared slightly younger. "My deepest apologies," Searel emotionless bowed to show respect; the resemblance was unmistakable—Searel's elder brothers.

"Mercer, are you ready to depart?" Rowan's gruff voice addressed the long-haired knight.

"I just wanted to see my dear baby brother off," A cruel smirk pulled at his lips. His eyes were a dull blue, not unlike Searel's.

He gripped the hem of his shirt as though he was preparing to drag him along. "Let's just go," The short-haired knight glared intently at Mercer,

"Ever the impatient one, Auden," Mercer cooed as he backed away from Searel, releasing the hem of his neckline. "Guess we can't soil our hands with these worms," he mocked while departing with Rowan and Auden.

"You're such a coward," Aver said through gritted teeth; the truth in the matter was that he was no better than Searel. He could not oppose his father any more than Searel could oppose his brothers. "I assure you I am," he paused momentarily.

"Now, come your highness, you should rest in your quarters," his hand on Aver's shoulder. He let out a sigh in defeat; there was no point in arguing with Searel; he was as stubborn as a stone. And would likely accept any harsh word uttered to him. *"His brothers were members of the elite king's guard, and they never let Searel forget it; while they were guarding the king and the realm, Searel was relegated to me. When I became a knight, he, too, remained by my side. And someday, when I take my rightful place on the throne, I'll topple those fools of the king's guard, and Searel will take his rightful place next to my throne."* Aver thought to himself.

Aver watched from the balcony overlooking the castle entrance as Rowan, Auden, and Mercer mounted their horses and set out to Deorad. A look of poignant disgust was plain on his face. "What kind of a Crown Prince does nothing for his people?" Aver bitterly muttered to himself.

A wicked thought crossed his mind, and he began pacing. He could use this as an opportunity to prove to his father that he was ready to ascend the throne.

Aver was nineteen. His father was twenty when he ascended the throne. Aver was confident in the scheme he had concocted; he would take Searel, and they would follow the king's guard to Deorad. It's not like Rowan or the lot of them had even seen the mage. Searel and he knew what he looked like; all they had to do was find him first, then he could leave the head of that monster at his father's feet.

Aver walked briskly to the ornate doors that decorated his large room; Searel was probably where he always was, Aver thought to himself. He began walking to the kingdom's library, and there he sat slumped against a statue, a book open before him. "Let's go, Searel; we have a score to settle in Deorad," Searel rose from the base of the statue, depositing the book he was reading gently behind him, "as you wish, Your Highness," a look of annoyance plain on his face. Searel straightened the sword at his side. Aver cast a condescending look toward the castle entrance as he turned on his heels and started towards it,

Searel in tow.

10

Lessons in Uncursing Oneself

Leona felt something tickling the tip of her nose as she scrunched her face in annoyance. One green eye opened, revealing Felle pushed up on a chair near the bed. He was leaning against the chair with his legs elegantly crossed as he dangled a bright blue feather mere inches from Leona's face. Her crimson hair spilled over her face in messy waves. She sat up and scowled.

Felle let out a bright laugh. "Good Afternoon, Cursed Princess," His smile was lovely and entirely out of place on his usually apathetic face.

"Why are you in such a good mood?" Leona asked, rubbing sleep from her eyes. Felle extended his hand and pinched a small piece of parchment between his middle and pointer fingers. He offered it to Leona. She took it and immediately unfolded it to reveal its contents.

"Adira sent me to gather supplies. I'm sure you won't listen to my warnings, but for the love of Caillte, stay away from Felle.

Yours, Dean"

Leona felt disappointment wash over her reading Dean's letter. *"He couldn't wait for me to wake?"* Leona thought to herself. No wonder Felle was elated; they sure did seem to get on each other's nerves. Dean was so against Felle being in the same place as her that he had to specify it in his letter. Come to think of it; Dean wasn't the only one missing; Mars was nowhere to be seen either. Perhaps Dean took her with him.

"Leona, I don't mean to be cross, but" Felle looked at her with sincerity, "How do you plan to learn magic from that human?" His question was devoid of sarcasm; instead, concern seemed to creep into his words.

"I didn't know how to curse myself, and somehow I managed to do that," she uttered, embarrassment plain on her face.

"Please, promise me something," Felle met her gaze and clasped her hand gently, "If you cannot undo what you have done. You will return with me to The Isles of your own will," Felle's words surprised Leona; he was back to being a completely different person when they were alone, a more serious and gentler being, a true departure from his usual cold and chaotic demeanor.

"I promise," the words barely a whisper. Leona did not want to die; however, she had no desire to relegate the rest of her days to The Isles. Ruling Caillte aside, she could never separate herself from the bonds she held so dear, like those that tied her and Mars together or her father and Dean. Although they differed, Leona could never imagine life without the ones she cared so deeply for.

"The Siren mage wished for you to meet her by the cliffs when you awoke," Felle looked away as he spoke, not wanting to meet Leona's eyes. She wondered if he would have told her that if she had not promised to return to The Isles if she failed. "The familiar is with her," he uttered. Leona had heard him address Mars as such before; she had never heard that word before, Felle.

"Why do you call Mars a familiar?" Leona asked,

"That's what she is," Felle responded flatly.

"What is a familiar anyway?" Leona asked, confusion clear in her voice.

"They are spirits tied to blood pacts," Felle did not elaborate further; he stood and began going to the door.

"I don't understand, Felle. Mars has always been with me," Leona's voice was filled with confusion and a hint of sadness. Felle looked at Leona over his shoulder and said, "Perhaps I am not the one you should ask," His words left Leona with a pit in her stomach. He was always so cryptic.

"The Sirens mage left this for you," Felle tossed a bundle of fabric at Leona and walked through the door to the hall. She examined the wad of fabric and realized it was a dress. Leona smoothed it out; it was an intricately woven black dress with white sleeves and brass cuffs. Her fingers trailed along the delicate details. It was an expertly made dress, not like the ones in Caillte; the gown Adira left for her was tailored for movement and practicality instead of indulgence and frills.

The dress was elegant yet lightweight and flexible. Leona slipped the shimmering gown she had been wearing from The Isles above her slender arms and plopped it onto the wooden floor of the cottage. She quickly replaced the gown with the one Adira had left her. A small pair of black boots was on the nightstand next to the bed. Leona slipped them on, and miraculously, they fit relatively well as she laced them tightly.

Leona departed the cottage; her hair blew against the breeze as she hit the cobblestone path. The sunlight was bright, and although the breeze was gentle, there was a slight haze in the area. The salty smell of the ocean permeated her senses as she made her way through the sleepy town of Siren, following the winding path that led to the cliffs by the sea.

The hillside was green, and large rocks scattered throughout it. In the distance, Leona spotted silver hair blowing delicately in the ocean air near the rocks that littered the shore. "Adira!" Leona shouted. She turned, a kind smile on her face as she enthusiastically waved.

"Took you long enough, kid," Adira placed her hands on her hips and regarded Leona. "Those fit you like a glove," Pride was apparent in her tone.

"Thank you. I've never worn such an intricate dress before," Leona ran her fingers along the hem of the skirt, which fell just past her knees.

"You're too kind. I'm sure Cyrus had you dripping in jewels and satin," Adira remarked. Leona let out an awkward smile. Leona felt fur gently rub against her leg, and she looked down to see Mars nuzzling her.

"Mars!" Leona bent down and scooped her into a hug. Her fur gently tickled Leona's cheek as she embraced Mars.

Mars was Leona's safe place; Mars was still not quite herself, though Leona thought it best not to probe. After their embrace, Mars elegantly leaped from her arms and sat at her feet.

"I have some people you should meet," Adira pulled Leona's attention back to the task at hand, "If you are to learn magic, it's best you learn from those who readily possess it," Leona was anxious as Adira let out a loud whistle.

From behind a large rock near the shore walked a group of some of the most breathtakingly beautiful women Leona had ever seen.

"This is Synth," Adira gestured to the group's first woman. Her long and flowing hair was an inky black, and her eyes were a piercing and intense red. Her skin shone like crystals in the sunlight; her thin frame was elegantly clothed in a flowing parchment-colored dress with a slit.

"The blonde one next to her is Meldy," Adira gestured to a shorter woman with long, flowing blond hair and intense red eyes. Her skin had the same diamond-like sheen as Synth's, and she flashed a bright smile at Leona, revealing a perfect set of teeth. She was clothed in a more intricate dress with pearls stitched along the hem of the green fabric.

"The pink-haired one is Lyra," Adira gestured to the final woman, who stood further back from the first two. Her hair was long and flowing like the others, the color of cherry blossoms, and her eyes piercing red. She wore a simple white, long-sleeved gown that was corseted along her waist.

"Hello," Leona shyly uttered to the three. "My, that is a rather nasty curse you've cast," Lyra spoke in an almost musical voice. "Yes, it is," Adira concurred, "Can you ladies help her?". Lyra, Synth, and Meldy exchanged knowing looks; they were silent momentarily, "I suppose we can try," Lyra uttered.

"I didn't know so many mages lived this far from Caillte," Leona excitedly mused.

"Silly girl, we aren't mages; we're of the sea," Meldy let out a giggle as she beamed at Leona.

"I don't understand," Leona was confused.

"We're the deities of the sea," Synth chimed in.

"Or, in plain words, they're sirens," Adira said.

A look of shock crossed Leona's face as Meldy clasped her

hand and began to pull her to the water that lapped at the shoreline. Mars gave Leona a worried look as Adira knelt next to her, ruffling her ears. The moment Meldy's shimmering skin touched the water, beautiful scale patterns etched on her porcelain-like skin. She pulled Leona into the water, and as they trekked into the waves, Leona could feel warmth envelop her.

Meldy began to hum; *come to the waves where the rocks meet the sea, and the sand and the trees sway; come to the water deep, where the sea breathes her breath, and the shore fades away from your eyes.* Meldy's lyrical voice was haunting; Leona could feel her legs begin to move further on their own as if every word drew her closer to the heart of the sea. The water now passed Leona's waist and started lapping up her chest.

"What's happening?" Leona began to panic as the words had no sound as they tried to fall from her lips. Meldy continued to sing her melody, forcing Leona deeper into the waves. She could feel a haze wash over her.

Leona was under the water in the blink of an eye; the shore felt as though it had given way beneath her. Fathomless waves surrounded her. She let out a scream as the air escaped her lungs, her fingers clawing at her throat in desperation. Was she going to die? Fear threatened to consume Leona as she clawed at her throat, desperate for air, for help. Her eyes began to flutter closed as she felt the weight of the water like a thousand stones on her chest, pulling her deeper. How can this be the end?

"I want to live,"

Light erupted from the water below. Leona's eyes shone through the water, almost as if the darkness and haze that had flooded her senses were being lifted, she gave way to the feeling and felt warmth course through her body. In a burst of water as though the ocean had expelled her, the water exploded along the shoreline; Leona lay beneath it, soaked from the salty water that had just swallowed her.

A searing pain pulled her attention to her wrist; the inky black thorns began to twist and creep further up her arm. Tears pooled in her eyes as she began to scream.

"Fight through it!" Adira screamed, her words piercing Leona's very core. Leona was powerless against the searing pain of her curse mark; it twisted and wound its way up her forearm; as she writhed, she heard the faint sound of what sounded like incantations.

The necklace Felle gave her cracked. The pain began to retreat slowly; unlike in her dream, the mark did not retreat. It remained burned into her skin. Leona began hyperventilating, her eyes full of betrayal as she gazed at Adira.

"Why?" her voice barely whispered.

"You have to get a handle on your magic; the fear of death is an excellent motivator," Adira said grimly. She knelt next to Leona, examining the spreading curse mark.

"It did work; you used magic to escape Meldy," Leona remembered the golden light surrounding her. Was that her magic? All she could think was that she wanted to live.

"You have to command your magic," Adira would not meet her eyes.

"Gosh, I'm sorry," a lyrical voice echoed behind Leona; it was Meldy. Her beautiful face was riddled with sadness.

"Adira was right," Leona uttered. "I have to fight through it," a look of determination apparent on Leona's face.

"Hit me with all you've got," Leona challenged. Adira felt a defiant smile tug at her lips. Reaching a hand to Leona, she pulled her to her feet in one fell swoop.

"As you wish," a smooth voice cooed. It was Synth. She began to form a blade with water from the waves. Her red eyes gazed at Leona before she took off in a sprint towards her, the water flowing sharply, taking on the shape of a sword.

Leona threw her arms up in defense, and the same warmth began coursing through her veins again; gold light erupted from her skin as the blade made contact, effectively disrupting its form, dissolving it back into formless water that dropped at Synth's feet. A look of triumphant shock was etched on Leona's face. Her green eyes were wide with disbelief. She was using magic.

11

Somewhere in Siren

"Thanks," Dean uttered to a man at a merchant stall; he was on the outskirts of Siren. The markets were near the tree line of the mountainside that divided Deorad. Although Siren was not a large capital like Deorad, it was still much larger than the first village they set out to after leaving the forest of Caillte. The bright-colored merchant stalls and shops lined the cobblestone paths, and Dean carefully kept his hood over his head.

Adira had told him there was no need for such paranoia in Siren. The royal knights hadn't been near the city for many years, and her alias was carefully safeguarded.

Adira had given him a bag of Yule and instructed him to find supplies for their journey ahead. He examined the parchment for the following item. Reading the list made him feel nostalgic for Caillte.

Adira's handwriting was strikingly similar to Cyrus's;

When he considered it, Adira and Cyrus seemed a lot alike.

They were both aloof and seemed to have vast amounts of knowledge at their fingertips. Perhaps that's why Cyrus told stories about Verona the Veracious to the children of the kingdom.

Dean felt melancholic as he thought back to the note he left for Leona. As much as he hated leaving her alone with Felle, he thought some distance would likely do them both good.

Things between them seemed to get more complicated and twisted the more time they spent together. Perhaps the distance Cyrus put between them in the first place sowed these seeds of doubt in him when it came to Leona. She herself had never betrayed his trust, and yet, he found himself turning into the very thing he hated so much from the others in Caillte.

Dean knew that it was unfair to put Leona in the position that he had been, that it wasn't her fault that she was royalty, and that she had gotten her hands on that grimoire. These were all choices that were made for her.

As much as he hated to admit it, Felle had helped Leona more than he had; stranger or not, he seemed to know a great deal. Dean pictured how Felle looked at Leona and felt anger bubble in his chest.

He didn't quite understand why it angered him so much that Felle seemed to take a certain liking to Leona; it wasn't as though she looked at him the same way back. Leona was still rather innocent when it came to how people regarded her.

Dean's attention was pulled back from his thoughts of Leona as he stared back at the parchment. He thought it best to continue procuring the items he needed so he could return to Leona's side. Even if she didn't want him there, he was determined to never leave her again; he would make this up to her.

The thought of Leona's smile burned into his mind. Her green eyes filled with a soft joy, and her laugh was like the sun after a long storm.

Dean couldn't find the words to describe the twisted mess of emotions he felt about Leona. He knew that when she was near, he felt like he was home. Did he need more than that? He wondered to himself. Did she need him the same way? A blush rose to his cheeks as he considered it. He shook it away as he continued going through the list.

The town of Siren seemed to have a certain charm. The people seemed carefree, and the sea air was something Dean had not expected to love so much. As he wandered through the crowd, his eyes caught sight of a mural painted onto the cobblestone wall between vendors. The mural depicted a woman sitting on the shore with a fishtail covered in scales. He had never seen such a strange depiction in Caillte.

"That's what this place is named for," An elderly merchant approached Dean, his hands clasped behind his slouching back. His clothes were plain, as appeared to be common for the area, and his wiry gray hair combed back against his aging skin.

"They say the first sailor who landed here encountered a magical deity with the voice of an angel and the form of a human and that of the ocean itself. It is said that the sailor had set out to sea before a great storm. The waves swallowed his ship, and the woman's voice led him to the safety of the shoreline. The town became known as Siren in honor of that act of mercy,"

Dean met his gaze, his eyes full of questions. "You worship the Sirens here?" the man laughed heartily at Dean's question.

"Long ago, that was the case; nowadays, it is more like they are respected and honored symbols of the land and sea," A thoughtful look in the man's eyes.

"I see," Dean wondered if the siren the man had long ago thought he saw could have been a mage instead.

"You aren't from around these parts, are you?" The man asked kindly, and Dean allowed a nervous look to pass his face.

"It's okay. We get a lot of travelers who settle here. Perhaps it is due to the magnetism the deities of the sea have bestowed upon this place,"

The man stood next to Dean as they both looked onward to the mural.

"I have a list of supplies I need to purchase; do you have some of them?" Dean thoughtfully asked the man. A warm smile spread across his face as he gestured toward a small merchant stall not too far away. Dean walked alongside him.

Dean examined the bag full of supplies. He double-checked the list that Adira had given him to make sure that everything was accounted for. The sun was beginning to wind down. It was not quite sundown, but Dean was certain that it would be soon.

He walked along the cobblestone path, admiring the stone cottages and shops that lined the paths. Siren was built like a cliff-side maze; down every street were twisting and winding side streets.

Although not as large as the capital city of Deorad, the town was still rather spread out. Dean caught his reflection in a shop window. His black hair was messy as it fell in his eyes. He looked around. Compared to the other people in the town, Dean seemed very out of place.

His black button-down shirt and fitted pants did not reflect the style of the human realm. There was a certain distinction in the way Caillte clothing were stitched, even the fabric seemed to differ from that of the non-magic regions. Dean's blue eyes seemed to twinkle as he gazed at the rushing waters in the distance.

"Deliver your messages yourself next time," a cold voice echoed behind him. Dean's face dropped as he saw Felle leaning against the cobblestone wall of a shop down the street.

"Why are you complaining? You've got to stay by her side," Dean bitterly glared at Felle. He walked toward Dean and bent ever so slightly to bring his face to eye level with Dean.

"I don't desire to deliver disappointments to her," A condescending look in his steely blue eyes. "Next time, do it with your own hand. Coward," Dean could feel rage bubble inside of him along with embarrassment; he broke Felle's gaze and stepped back. Dean bit his tongue and started back toward the tavern. *"Why does he think he can say whatever he wants to me?"* Dean fumed.

He had no desire to give Felle the reaction he was seeking. After a few moments, Dean looked back; Felle had disappeared. *He calls me a coward, yet he is the one who runs away.*

12

Chasing Ghosts

The wind blew Felle's long hair behind him; he watched from the top of the cliffside as Leona endured her turbulent trials to try and muster an ounce of control of the magic energy that ran through her veins.

He sat at the edge of the rocks above, his legs sprawled before him as he leaned back. Seeing Dean in the town filled Felle with contempt. He thought Dean to be a cowardly child. Felle's torments of Dean were not merely for entertainment; he genuinely disliked the boy. He thought him to be useless, not just to Leona but also to Felle's plans for her. If anything, he thought him a great hindrance.

Felle had no reservations about removing Dean from his path if it weren't for Leona's devotion to the little idiot. He scowled in discontent.

His eyes were on the waves ahead, and the ocean air was a familiarity Felle had not experienced in over twenty years. His blue eyes were quick to detect the motion at the edge of his vision.

"Hello, familiar," Felle's words had a hint of sadness in them as he addressed Mars.

"Did you tell her?" Mars asked softly.

"No," Felle uttered; a look of sadness washed over him.

"Why do you not speak to her?" Felle questioned,

"I don't wish to lie to her," Mars replied honestly,

"Seems as though she has that effect on others," Felle uttered.

"She's a lot like Vyes, in all the worst ways," Mars fondly reflected.

"Did she suffer in the end?" Felle let the words escape his lips; Mars sat beside Felle, overlooking the cliffs.

"No," Mars uttered softly. Mars gazed as Felle's usually emotionless face was painted with sadness.

"Will you tell her?" Felle's eyes met Mars,

"I haven't decided," Mars replied sincerely. The wind blew gently around them. Felle's usual sarcastic and snarky demeanor was completely gone.

"When I've fulfilled my promise, will you swear a promise to me?" Mars asked Felle in a soft voice.

"I'll swear the same promise you swore to Vyes," Felle uttered "I'll keep it till the end," his words were sincere. Mars felt the anxiety that had been twisting in her since Felle encountered them in Deorad fall away.

She no longer stood terrified in the face of the truth, Felle would not reveal this long-sworn pact to Leona, nor would he interfere in Vyes wishes. The same fondness he felt for Vyes was not lost on her daughter.

"She promised to return to The Isles if this fails," Felle softly stated; a look of momentary shock crossed Mars's face,

"I do not believe she will fail," Mars countered.

"She could..." Felle's words were laced with a quiet hope, Mars was not surprised. Leona was the last thing tying the memory of Vyes to this realm. Leona shared the same long flowing red hair and forest green eyes as Vyes; they were not unalike in spirit either. For all their similarities, they were also very different; Leona was much softer than Vyes, and she was kind to a fault.

"She is not Vyes Felle," Mars softly stated.

"I know..." Felle's words were barely a whisper.

"Perhaps it's time we stop chasing ghosts," Mars said, making her way down the cliffside back to the shoreline.

Felle had no desire to "chase ghosts," nor did he want to relive the memories of his failures. He was a selfish man, and he knew this of himself well. Leona may not be Vyes, but being near her threatened to tear his heart asunder. He desperately wanted to keep her near.

Perhaps it is the hope in her eyes.

If she returned with him to The Isles, he could assure that no harm would ever befall even a single hair upon her head. A soft smile made its way to his lips as he overlooked the ocean waves.

Being here reminded him of then. A memory flashed into his mind of Vyes standing at the very same cliffside, her long crimson hair billowing in the wind behind her, her green eyes ablaze with wonder. Felle remembered embracing her, his lips softly pressed against hers. Twenty years later, the only woman to ever bring color to his life was long dead. Her daughter was tethered to a curse that threatened to consume her. Things would be different this time, Felle would not fail, not again.

The sunset was present at the end of the long expanse of

water. Leona had retreated to the tavern with the others. Felle's concern for Leona was apparent as he considered the odds of her success, the curse mark had already begun spreading further up her arm. If she continued to use magic with no direction there was no telling what may result from it.

Felle considered telling Leona that her efforts were in vain and taking her back to The Isles, however, he doubted she would take his word for it and abandon her resolve to push through. She had no idea what she was doing. On the off chance that she was able to give her magic form, she would likely not return to The Isles. Felle pondered the possibility; a quiet resolve washed over him as the ocean air danced around him gently. Whether she succeeded or not, he fully intended to remain near to her for as long as he could.

As Felle made his way back to the tavern, he thought about how different the world seemed after only a short while. The last time he had been in Siren, there was not nearly the same presence of humans. The soft light of the tavern illuminated the cobblestone path ahead of him. He leaned against the side of the building, feeling his head touch the cold stone as he closed his eyes.

"I'm surprised you didn't interfere," Adira's cold tone cut through the otherwise serene evening. Felle's intense eyes met Adira's cool silver ones. "And if I had?" he uttered with his arms crossed, still leaning against the side of the tavern wall.

Adira gave him an icy glare. "You don't remember me, do you?" she spat the words at Felle.

"All you humans look the same," he scoffed. Adira's silver hair bellowed around her; the evening air was cool. The winter solstice would bring the snow, and although summer had just ended, she could feel it as the seasons began to shift.

"I suppose I shouldn't be surprised. You did only ever have eyes for her," She looked at Felle with a face of resigned defeat and a hint of sadness behind her steely eyes.

A look of realization fell across Felle's usually emotionless face. He dropped his arms, and as if seeing the woman before him with new eyes, he remembered her. In an instant, the image of a young girl no older than fifteen flashed in his memory, with her long silver hair and gray eyes.

Although it had been eighteen years since he laid his eyes upon her, the woman before him, with her long silver hair billowing gently in the wind and cold silver eyes, could not be mistaken. "Celia?" Felle uttered, surprised. "I don't use that name anymore," A sad smile pulled at her lips. "You're the siren mage?" Felle was in disbelief. "Why are you not with that idiot?" he said contemptuously. She softly chuckled,

"My brother exiled me to the human realm the day Vyes passed on. Guess he didn't want a walking reminder of the past," Her smile was filled with sadness. Felle felt the embers of his rage for Cyrus begin to ignite again.

"Leona doesn't know, so how about you do me a favor for old times' sake and keep this between us?" She pursed her lips and held her finger over them; her gray eyes were no longer the light-hearted ones of a child. Felle let out a deep sigh. His black hair billowed gently, and his blue eyes shone brightly, filled with the moon's first light.

"Why are you all so content to lie to her?" Felle questioned.

"You're not exactly telling her the truth either," Adira replied, annoyed.

"I have told her more truth than you or your idiot brother has," he spat at her.

"Well, Felle, she's still a child. The less she knows, the better.

Look at the mess she already made," Adira asserted

"The responsibility of her curse lies solely on the false king's shoulders. Had he not lied to her about her true nature, perhaps she wouldn't have sought out a grimoire," Felle blamed Cyrus not only for Vyes' undoing but also for Leona's curse.

"What are you playing at here?" Adira challenged, her eyes burning with curiosity and the undertones of anger.

"She will awaken, and when she does, we will return to The Isles," Felle stated plainly.

Adira let out a cruel laugh.

"Perhaps the most foolish one here is you. She will never abandon the human realm to be but a bird in a cage," Adira knew that comparing The Isles to little more than a birdcage was an unfair assertion. As much as she wanted to poke holes in Felle's plans, she knew that he did not mean any harm to Leona. Instead, he was a desperate man consumed by guilt.

"Think what you want, human," Felle averted his gaze as he pushed off the wall and headed into the tavern.

Felle did not feel like arguing with the likes of her; she could think what she wanted, and it was of no consequence to Felle. Leona had already given him her word, and he intended to hold her to it whether she meant it or not.

As he made his way through the tavern to the back opening of the cottage, he opened Leona's door ever so slightly; she was sprawled out on the bed, her pale skin etched with the inky black tendrils of thorns that had now crept their way up her arm. The necklace Felle had given her was emanating a weaker aura than before.

Felle's eyes observed Leona's exhausted form; her long crimson hair was spilled out around her, and he could hear the faint sound of her breathing while she was asleep. He could not believe that someone so stubborn could sleep soundly and carefree.

"Enjoying the show?" Dean's voice echoed behind Felle.

"She has such lovely skin, don't you think? A girl like her should really be careful not to leave so much of it, or she may catch a cold," Felle smirked cruelly as he teased Dean. Dean's face turned a bright shade of pink as he stammered, "Y-y-you're unbelievable," He angrily pushed past Felle and pulled Leona's door closed. He was glaring intently at Felle.

Felle laughed at Dean's reaction. He leaned against the door frame and met Dean's gaze. Felle's serpent-like eyes had a playful aura.

"Tell me, boy," Felle clicked his tongue. "Do you intend to protect her or possess her?" His words surprised Dean.

"I-I have sworn to protect Leona as a knight of Caillte, and that means I will do what I must to bring her home," Dean said with conviction.

"So, it's possession," Felle uttered; Dean was taken aback at the assertion.

"I didn't say that!" Dean exclaimed

"You didn't need to," Felle leaned in. "I can see right through you," With his hands tucked into his jacket pockets, he let out a chuckle and walked right past and into the adjoining room, leaving Dean speechless in the hall for the second night in a row. *"I really hate that kid,"* Felle thought to himself.

13

What is Ordered, What is Just

Rowan and the king's guard departed the Kingdom of Aims the following night to seek out the mage who had gotten away in Deorad. Rowan, Auden, and Mercer were none the wiser that behind them, a mile back, trailed Aver and Searel.

They had made it to Deorad, and within the city's bustle, Aver could easily slip into the crowd with Searel. They took the servant horses instead of their usual steeds to avoid suspicion.

If the king had found out that Aver so blatantly disobeyed a direct order, Aver was certain his father would use it to further prevent him from ascending the throne.

Deorad was as it was the day they trailed the mage; the buildings had still not been repaired, although the citizens seemed to be recovering from the calamity that befell them.

"Searel," Aver's voice was quiet; he did not desire to draw any attention to them. Searel followed Aver down an alleyway in the great city and peeked out so he could observe them from a distance.

"I don't think they would recognize you even if we ventured closer," Searel said with an emotionless look on his face. His long white hair and dull eyes were shrouded by a cloak concealing his knight's armor.

"I'm not going to take any chances with those dead-eyed idiots and that self-righteous prick," Aver spat the words. He was clothed in the same long cloak that concealed his armor underneath; the hood pulled up fell near his eyes, perfectly averting his golden hair and shrouding him.

In the distance, Rowan and the king's guard began to confront the citizens of the kingdom. His serious face took in every detail as he sketched on a piece of parchment; it seemed as though he was getting eyewitness accounts to create a composite sketch to identify the mage.

"Dammit," Aver clenched his teeth. At this rate, they would find the mage before Aver or Searel had so much as a chance to interrogate him.

As Aver continued observing the men, he noticed that they appeared to have gathered a fair amount of information. He ventured closer, careful not to raise any suspicion. His back was turned to the crowd being questioned. He set his eyes on a small vendor stall and craned his neck to try and listen to the crowd's murmurs.

"I saw him! He had eyes like a snake!" a woman yelled amongst the crowd.

"He was going to the woods!" another yelled.

"That over there is a Siren; I heard there's a mage there!" a man added.

Aver had heard all he needed; he retreated to the alleyway.

"Searel, let's go," he ordered, setting off down the opposing alleyway toward the city's heart.

"Did you hear anything of importance?" Searel questioned

"The Sirens mage is connected to this one," Aver looked at Searel over his shoulder, "We'll put an end to that devil and show up those idiots in the process," He had a proud smirk painted on his face. His golden eyes ablaze with conviction.

Aver and Searel quietly slipped out of the city before Rowan and the king's guard could.

On the road to Siren, Aver noticed that the thick, lush forest and mountain dividing Deorad was an area that was known to be forbidden due to the presence of poisonous plants and animals that resided in it.

A thought crossed his mind; he wondered if the mage had cast a spell to poison the humans who dared to enter it.

"Such evil creatures," Aver muttered to himself.

He and Searel soon found themselves entering the cliffside that wound Siren.

"Still no sign of Rowan and the idiot brigade," Aver uttered smugly to Searel.

"We should still hurry," Searel grimaced.

"Shut up, Searel," Aver glared at him as he dismounted his horse. They had found a few trees just outside the forest dividing the mountain from Siren, where they tied their horses. It had only been half a day's journey from Deorad; even so, Aver had no desire to have his face off with Rowan until he held the mage in his hand.

The two made their way into the city; as they looked around, Aver was surprised to see that they had so many vendors in such a small town. The cliffs overlooked an expansive ocean. The breeze blew his hood down, revealing his golden hair, the sun's rays cascading into his golden eyes. As if pulled by an unnamed force, his eyes caught sight of a tall man with long black hair blowing behind him, rounding the corner near the cliffs below.

"Searel!" Aver shouted at him as he broke out into pursuit of the figure.

Searel broke into a sprint down the winding alleyways of Siren. He pulled a dagger from a sheath on his thigh and had it poised, ready to slash. Aver was closely in tow, his sword not drawn yet.

Aver ran through the cobblestone streets down to the shore below. The tall man stood, clad in black, his hair blowing gently in the breeze. He looked at them over his shoulder, his icy blue eyes ablaze with a cold rage.

Searel charged at him and tried to slash him with his dagger; the man sidestepped his attack instantly, completely unfazed.

Aver drew his sword, the metal gleaming in the sun. Aver lunged at the man, and he was pushed back as the wind whipped around him.

"I'm here to slay the siren mage in the name of the Kingdom of Aims!" Aver yelled each word, dripping with conviction.

A twisted smile pulled at the man's lips,

"Are you prepared to die for your kingdom?" his cold eyes met Aver's.

"As the Crown Prince, I will lay down my life for my people!" With that last assertion, Aver lunged once again.

Aver slashed at the wall of wind, blocking his attacks. The man simultaneously began forming blades out of the water and hurling them with a mere flick of his wrist at him and Searel. They both continued their attack. Out of the corner of Aver's eye, he caught sight of the gleam of a sword; before he could fully react, steely blue eyes and a flash of black hair had contacted his sword. The clinging of swords drowned out Searel's words as realization poured over them: the boy who was locked in battle with Aver was the same one they had seen in Tearn.

"Aver, fall back!" Searel desperately yelled. One of the water blades tore through his cheek, barely missing his eye.

The boy's constant and quick slashes were not those of a novice. Aver was struggling to match his pace. He furiously continued pushing Aver back. His sword was drawn, and his eyes met Aver's golden ones.

"I don't wish to kill you. But I will," each word dripping with malice.

Aver smirked proudly,

"Try me, demon," he challenged.

With that provocation, their swords made contact once again.

Before Aver knew it, Searel was on the ground, and the tall man clad in black beckoned Searel's blade to him. In an instant, he held it in his hand and turned the blade toward Searel. Without thinking, Aver's feet moved beneath him.

Hot, searing pain penetrated his chest as the knife tore through his chest plate and into his ribs. "Aver!" Searel let out a feral scream.

Instantly, a blaze of flames licked up the cliffside, and the sky began to take on a fire glow. Aver's vision began to cloud, but in the distance, he could make out Rowan's stern, scarred face as he threw a torch into a nearby home, engulfing it in flames.

"S-save the people, you idiot!" Aver commanded Searel through gritted teeth.

The tall man clad in black turned his attention to the cliffside as he strode to face the king's guard; the boy who had fought Aver followed suit.

Light emanated from the edge of his boots and the hilt of his blade as the boy followed the tall man clad in black. Aver wondered momentarily as the edges of his vision began to haze if the boy's magic was why he was beaten so easily or if he was as weak as he felt. The look of malice in his blue eyes was somehow familiar.

14

Seeds of Rebellion

The acrid smell of flames awoke Leona, she quickly pulled herself to her feet and searched for Mars. Her eyes were blurry from the smoke; she had no idea what time it was. The last thing she remembered was hearing Felle and Dean tell Adira they were going out. Panic began to rise in Leona. She could feel something horrible on the horizon; she slipped her boots on and pushed her way out of the tavern.

There was no sign of anyone; flames and black clouds of smoke painted the sky, deafening the light of the sun. She began to run through the winding alleyways towards the cliffside.

The buildings, homes, and shops were ablaze; the entire town was burning.

In the distance, Leona heard metal clanging. She followed the sound to the shoreline. Her emerald eyes pricked with tears; Dean was locked in battle with knights of the human kingdom alongside Felle. Leona tried to let out a scream but was pulled back by a small hand covering her mouth and tugging her down behind the cliffs on the shore. Lyra's red eyes were frantic. Behind her, Meldy and Synth cowered.

"What's happening?" Leona was frantic.

"The knights attacked when they saw him standing on the shore, and then more joined." Lyra was terrified.

"Where is Adira!" Leona exclaimed through heavy breaths.

"She went to evacuate the townspeople," Lyra softly uttered

The sound of metal clashing rang out.

"I have to do something," Leona closed her eyes and put her hands out; golden light began to emanate from her hands.

In an instant, the black mark that was creeping up her arm began to tighten, and searing pain burned away at her senses. Leona let out a scream. Lyra covered her mouth to muffle the noise.

"We'll only get in the way!" Meldy said with tears in her red eyes

Lyra gently caressed Meldy and Synth's cheeks, "Take her and run," She pulled her hair from its pin, and the pink waves fell around her.

"I'm sorry I couldn't do more," She smiled sadly and walked out from the corner of the cliff.

Leona crawled after her and peered around the side of the cliff.

Lyra approached a knight with long white hair who was tending to an injured knight. The knight's blond hair was streaked with blood as he lay unconscious on the sandy shores.

"Get out of here! The flames will swallow this village!" The white-haired man exclaimed. Lyra knelt before him, caressed his face between her thin fingers, and placed her lips on his; he was too shocked by her actions to react. Her red eyes glowed,

117

and the knights' dull ones took on the same shade of red.

"Fight for me," she uttered softly.

The knight immediately rose to his feet, pulled his sword from his sheath, and started approaching the battle ensuing between Felle, Dean, and the three other knights.

Leona's breath caught in her throat, and the sight of Felle and Dean fighting outnumbered made her feel entirely powerless.

From what she could see, it seemed that the knight Lyra bewitched, and the one bleeding on the shore was not with the three who were in a battle with Felle and Dean. The flashing sparks from their swords contacting made Leona's heartbeat ever faster.

"Well, if it isn't our little brother," a mocking voice cooed.

Leona saw a long white-haired knight that looked strikingly like the knight Lyra had bewitched approach from the commotion.

"Don't worry, brother, I'll make sure you have a blessed funeral," a cruel smile on his face.

The two nights began their battle, and Lyra's red eyes were glowing. She made her way to the higher cliffs where Felle and Dean were.

Leona began to move and felt a small hand grip her wrist. Meldy and Synth, both with tear-filled eyes, peered at her.

"I'm going to help her; you need to run," Leona assured them.

The two looked at her through tears and nodded. Leona sprinted to the shoreline, her red hair blowing around her. The smoke had intensified in the few moments she spent addressing Meldy and Synth. She couldn't see in front of her; only the sound of metal clanking and the occasional sparks would be visible through the thick clouds of smoke.

A searing burn caught Leona's arm, and she instinctively

grabbed at her skin; when she pulled her hand away, blood dripped from her fingers. Panic began to rise in her. She was defenseless. *Whish* another flash of searing pain broke out on her thigh, Leona let out a cry. On the ground next to her was a small, thin blade coated in her blood.

"Get out of here!" Felle's voice penetrated the smoke, and her eyes found his silhouette through the smoke as he continued fighting.

"I'll fight too!" she grabbed the thin blade that had cut her and wrapped both her dainty hands around it. *Whish,* another slash rang out from the smoke. Felle stumbled back as he looked at Leona over his shoulder. Before he could stop it, another blade was thrown.

Leona closed her eyes in anticipation of the pain.

Clink

She tore her eyes open; standing before her was a tall knight, his golden hair streaked with blood.

"I...won't let my people die..." his voice was weak.

This knight had just protected her. His body wavered, whether from the blood loss or the smoke, Leona couldn't discern. He slumped back into her.

"Leave Leona! You'll only get in the way!" Dean's voice rang out from the smoke and flames.

In resigned defeat, Leona braced the wavering knight against her and began lumbering toward the tree line by the edge of the cliffs. Tears began to fall from her eyes. She felt entirely useless. How could she leave them there to fight alone?

The flames continued to lick their way into the mountainside, and Leona was slowly evading them. She could have gotten further in if it weren't for the weight of this knight. She couldn't just leave him there to die, especially after he had tried to help her, even at the cost of himself.

There was a small clearing ahead, near a pond; Leona could still see the glow of the fire in the distance. Some stones were inlaid into a small cave-like structure. She gently set the knight down and started examining his wound.

Her delicate fingers gently removed his breastplate. She let out a gasp. There was so much blood pouring from the wound in his ribs. Leona gazed at his face in panic. His breathing was shallow, a band of sweat clear on his brow.

She quickly tore at the dress Adira had given her in a crude attempt at making gauze. She began applying pressure to the wound. "Ahh," he gritted his teeth in pain.

"I-I'm sorry," Leona softly murmured as she tried to slow the bleeding.

"Please, please, let me repay the kindness of this stranger," as if silently praying.

Leona felt warmth in the tips of her fingers as she continued to apply pressure to the gaping hole in his ribs.

A soft golden light began to glow from the wound; the bleeding was slowing, and this man's pained expression seemed to give way to relief in his features.

Once the feeling of warmth had stopped, she gently removed the blood-soaked cloth from his chest. The wound had closed. Leona's eyes widened in shock. She turned her attention to her arm, where the searing thorns resided. However, they did not continue to climb higher. They stayed where they were.

Leona quickly gathered herself and tore off more fabric from her dress. She then went to the stream and began to wet it. When she returned, she gently placed it upon the knight's head.

She gazed at him. His eyes were still closed, and he didn't appear to be in much pain anymore. His armor bore the crest of the Kingdom of Aims. His blond hair was streaked with blood, and his armor was soaked with it.

Leona wasn't sure how much time had passed like that as she gently tended to him. She noticed the glow of the fire had dimmed a bit in the distance; the smoke was just as thick, however.

"Where am I?" a hoarse voice uttered.

Leona looked shocked. His eyes fluttered open gently, revealing golden irises, and Leona was in awe of their beauty.

"I-uh brought you to the forest," She stammered.

He attempted to push himself up but quickly fell back down.

"Stop! You need to rest!" Leona gently pushed him down.

"I have to save my people," he groaned through pain as he tried to push himself up again.

"You were hurt badly," Leona uttered gently.

"I have to stop Searel...His brothers will kill him," he uttered through clenched teeth.

"You can't move; you'd only get in the way," Leona said bitterly

He clenched his fist and hit it against the ground.

His blond hair fell in his eyes as he averted his gaze. After a moment, Leona lifted her eyes to him; his hair obscured his face, but the look of twisted shame on his face was still visible to her eyes.

"Those dear to me are fighting too..." Leona spoke softly

His expression softened. His eyes fell upon the inky black curse mark on Leona's arm, and a look of anger flashed in his eyes.

"If I wasn't so weak, I could've stopped this..." his words were dripping with contempt.

Leona followed his gaze to her curse mark. She quickly shifted her arm to behind her and out of sight.

"It's not what you think," she said sheepishly.

"You got cursed by one of those devils I allowed to get away in Deorad." He said resignation in his voice.

A look of shock crossed Leona's face.

"No, someone didn't curse me; I–" he cut her off,

"You don't have to hide it; you didn't do anything wrong. It's my fault." A defeated smile crossed his lips.

"How can it be your fault when you don't even know me," Leona said with conviction.

"As the Crown Prince of Aims and a royal knight of the kingdom, it is my oath to protect all those who reside in the land from the pitfalls of evil," he said sadly.

Leona looked at him understandingly. She knew what it felt like to carry the responsibility of all your people, and even if it didn't make logical sense to do so, she could empathize with him. However, she was certain that he would likely turn on her as soon as she revealed the truth to him.

"Why did you protect me...?" she asked softly.

"Because it's my duty. What kind of knight allows an unarmed woman to be shredded to pieces before him?" He spoke softly.

After a moment of silence, Leona pushed her hand out and introduced herself. "I'm Leona." His golden eyes met hers. The color in his face was slowly beginning to return.

"I'm Aver," he uttered as he shook her hand firmly. Leona thought he was relatively strong even for being incapacitated mere moments before.

He pointed at her curse mark, "Now that I know your name, how about you tell me how that happened?" he asked her seriously.

"The short version of it is, I have to learn how to use magic to undo it," Leona said plainly.

Aver looked stricken, like he had just been slapped.

"That's the craziest reasoning I have ever heard for seeking out magic," He uttered, surprised.

"I have to break my curse before the next full moon, so I don't have much time," Leona confided in him.

"How would learning the thing that did this to you help anything at all?" Aver questioned her, utterly confused.

"If I don't, I'll die." Leona averted her gaze.

A look of utter shock passed Aver's face. He let a defeated smile pull at his face. "Dammit." He uttered

15

A Knights Resolve

Thick smoke encased the sleepy seaside town as flames engulfed everything they touched. As the battle between Dean and the knights continued, Felle's attacks became increasingly uncontrolled. The black-haired knight who had been at the brunt of the assault was locked in a one-on-one with Felle.

Dean's eyes darted between him and the knight before him, his sword continued to let off sparks as it resounded against the knights. His short white hair and menacing eyes filled Dean with dread. These three were much stronger than the two he and Felle had fought on the shoreline.

In the distance, Dean caught sight of the long white-haired knight Felle had on the ground fighting with the other long-haired white knight from the upper cliffs. Dean had heard him call the man his brother, even though they were locked in a death match.

Although it was for a moment, Dean saw Lyra kiss the man before his eyes took on the same red hue as hers before he began fighting the other night. Dean knew they used magic, but he had never seen magic quite like that before.

In the heat of battle, he had instructed Leona to leave; although he regretted having to push her further away, he felt relief wash over him as he gazed at the shoreline and saw she was now gone.

Cling

The force of his sword meeting the other knights pulled him from his thoughts.

"Don't think we've forgotten about that little mouse you allowed to escape," the man said mockingly.

Dean felt rage rising within him. He struck the knight's sword with determined vigor.

"What's the matter, devil? Think we won't get her after we kill you?" the man seethed.

Dean could feel his face betray him as a look of rage and contempt fell upon it. The man smirked and pushed him back with the force of their swords connecting. Dean stumbled back and narrowly dodged the blade that struck a mere thread length next to him. He quickly blocked with his sword and jumped away before the next blow could connect.

As if walking in a circle, they continued this dance. Dean had never been so evenly matched against another knight.

In Caillte, he was the most skilled swordsman. However, this man, who appeared to be in his thirties, was just as skilled, if not more so, and the blood-lust was apparent in every strike. Even with his magic enhancing his speed and blade's hilt, the disparity remained between him and the knight.

"I won't die by your hand," Dean challenged as he lunged forward.

"Shut your mouth and fight, you idiot!" Felle yelled.

Felle's momentary distraction allowed Dean an opening.

In the blink of an eye, he struck with all his might, his blade connected with the knight's breastplate. The force of the impact flung him back.

"Auden!" yelled the other night with long hair that was locked in battle with the bewitched knight.

"End this, Mercer!" The knight fighting Dean replied. Before Dean could register, the man had come inches from his face and pierced the tip of his sword between the armor and Dean's shoulder. Blood splashed up as Dean rotated and dislodged it; he swiftly countered with a strike that contacted the knight's left eye, slicing it. He let out a scream as blood began to pour from the fingers that clasped his wound.

Upon hearing the scream, Mercer struck the bewitched knight and threw him back. He ran to the injured knight's side. "Brother!" He screamed as he braced the man against him and retreated towards the edge of the city. A pool of blood trailed behind them. Dean thought about pursuing them but resigned to assist Felle instead.

Out of the side of the smoke, Dean swung his blade at the dark-haired knight. He effectively dodged and hurled three small blades he had between his fingers at him in one movement. The blades pierced Dean before he could entirely dodge. Felle jumped in front of the knight and forced him back using his magic. He formed a blade from the embers around them. The firelight shone on Felle menacingly; his blue eyes reflected the burning flames around them.

"Move, boy," Felle growled. He lunged forward as the knight fearlessly began his assault once again. Felle's blade slashed the knight, and the impact caused everything around them to be pushed back, *clinging* to every hit. The sound rang out. They moved faster than Dean's eyes could detect in the smoke and flames.

He pulled the thin blades from his body, one from his leg and two from his injured shoulder.

In the distance, Dean could see Adira ushering the rest of the villagers into the nearby tree line above the cliffs. Mars was next to her. Dean could feel his chest tighten as he thought about Leona alone, injured and running for her life. He let out a silent prayer for her safety. When they reunited, he would ensure that he would not allow any more harm to come to her.

The clashing of blades was so intense that Dean could feel the temperature and air shift with each hit. He caught Felle's silhouette in the smoke as he approached the knight on the ground with his blazing sword. In another clink of the blades, the smoke dispersed. Felle jumped back, a cut bleeding on his emotionless face. The knight was not unscathed; however, he had a gaping wound gushing blood on his side.

He gritted his teeth and once again lunged for Felle. Dean drug himself up the cliffs and away from the debris flying as they continued their fight.

In a final burst, Felle's blade met the knights once again. The knight quickly threw three more thin blades; Felle dodged them as he jumped back; the knight used this opening to retreat into the smoke. Felle's eyes burned with rage as he chased after him into the smoke. The flames continued to burn the city to the ground. Dean looked around; all that remained of Siren would be ash.

16

An Eye for An Eye

Felle chased the knight into the heart of the flames, engulfing everything around him. Out of the corner of his eye, he saw the gleam of metal. He stepped to the side quickly and avoided it.

"Come forth, human," Felle challenged as he focused his magic to form a stone sword. He tilted it and straightened his stance, his eyes locked on the figure walking out from the smoke.

"I will add you to my collection when I finish you." The man coldly spoke. He held his sword in one hand and the other, a grimoire.

Felle's eyes burned with rage. He lunged forward, and a resounding shock echoed through the smoke.

His blade had been blocked by magic, the very magic Fae wielded that had imbued the grimoire in the knight's hand. He let out a cruel laugh.

"How does it feel! To be thwarted by the hand of your own kind, you demon!" He laughed as he continued to use the grimoire to block Felle's onslaught.

Felle straightened his sword, seething with malice.

"You would dare use the magic of the Fae against their king?" his eyes ablaze.

He let out a mocking laugh as he sized Felle up.

"I'll carve a crown into your skull after I've finished this." The man's eyes were cold; his face was scarred and harsh.

Felle's eyes began to glow a vibrant blue, and the flames around him began to stir, and with each step, his aura continued to grow. He could feel the power coursing through his veins. Behind him, a shadow began to take form; inky black wings spewed from his back in a twisted fashion; they were unnatural and gave off an air of unease. Felle's face was no longer emotionless; it was twisted in a cold rage, along his forehead, inky black thorns etched into his skin as though a cruel crown had been formed. His blade took on the same inky black hue.

His rage clouded his mind. An image of his people being slain flashed in his memory. With a flick of his wrist, he straightened his blade once again.

"Atone with your life." Felle lunged forward and shattered the magic shield that the knight had formed.

A look of shock crossed his face momentarily as he jumped back, evading his blade's slash. The knight's steel blade struck Felle's, and they began to clash again. Felle's movements were much quicker than earlier as he slashed away at the man. His blade wicked away the armor that clad his body. In an instant, Felle was propelled back. The man had another grimoire he began to use. This one had a familiar feeling to it. Felle could not quite place it; the magic in it was known to him.

"The filthy demon who imbued this one looked a lot like that little succubus that ran to the woods," He mockingly asserted.

Felle felt a cold rage wash over him as he realized why it was familiar. "She didn't have weird ears like him," he crudely pointed at his ears with a cruel smile curling on his lips.

"You'll die here." Felle would make no mistake. He would end this human, not just for what he had uttered of Leona but for the crimes he committed against his people. Felle remembered Vye's despair after her little brother was slain; they bore the same red hair and green eyes, and their magic was of the same nature.

Felle quickly slashed at the knight, each stroke increasing speed and veracity. In the blink of an eye, Felle plunged his blade through his armor and pierced him. Blood spurned from his mouth as Felle pulled his blade from him. A sadistic smile tugged at the knight's lips as he slumped to the forest floor. He instantly pulled another grimoire from his armor, and light enveloped the knight. Felle reached for him; his fingers barely grazed him before he was transported. Felle fell to his knees and clenched his empty fist as he screamed in rage. His eyes burned with anger; his magic continued to pour out, consuming the flames in black.

His slender fingers found his face as he buried his head in his hands. "How could I allow him to slip between my fingers!" he screamed the words. A hot rage coursed through him.

He knew without a doubt that Vye's little brother Ander had been forced to create that grimoire at some point. The magic was unmistakable. It was so familiar. The very incident that bathed her once carefree heart in despair was by the hand of that wretched human. Felle considered how he would tear him limb from limb the next time he encountered him.

In his turmoil, he thought of Leona; she was alone in these woods, and that knight could be in close pursuit of her. He slammed his fist into the ground, crushing the earth beneath it, and stood.

A new resolve washed over his face as the black wave of magic receded inside Felle. His wings dissolved in flicks of black, along with the crude crown etched into his forehead. His blue eyes shone against the first light of the moon. He had to find Leona before that human did. He would not allow her to meet the same fate that Ander and the rest of their people met by his hand. Without another thought, Felle turned, his cloak bellowed behind him, torn from the battle as he set out into the forest searching for Leona.

If she wasn't still alive by the time he found her, he was certain his wrath would consume him, and he would slaughter every last human he came upon.

17

The Burden of The Kingdom

The moon hung high and luminous in the night sky, its light casting a silvery sheen across the smoke-filled sky. The fire's glow had all but died out, but the scent of ash was still in the air. Aver slumped against the cold, jagged stone of the cave, the night air thick around them. Leona perched at the edge of the cave's entrance and absently traced circles in the dirt with a stick aimlessly.

"I'll probably regret asking you this, but—" Aver's voice broke the silence, and he tilted his head to look at Leona. Her eyes were fixed on the ground, avoiding his gaze. "Were you with those mages?" His golden eyes were sharp as he observed her, filled with a mix of curiosity and accusation.

"Were you with those psychos?" Leona uttered back defiantly.

Her gaze remained averted, her posture stiff. She shakily spoke, "I guess I'll have to live with your judgment, then."

Aver's eyes, still sharp, traced the curse mark that wound

around Leona's slender arm. His expression softened, and he let out a weary sigh, letting his head fall back against the stone. His blond hair, tousled and unkempt, framed his face in a disheveled halo.

"I guess I probably deserved that," he said, his voice carrying a hint of rueful acceptance. A faint, almost sad smirk tugged at the corners of his lips.

"Not all mages and magic are evil," Leona said quietly, her voice barely more than a whisper.

Aver's smile faded. His eyes hardened, and his words were short and final. "They are." The shift in his demeanor was palpable, his previous softness giving way to a cold certainty.

Leona's fingers stilled their restless tracing in the dirt, and she looked up, finally meeting Aver's gaze. Her emerald and troubled eyes held his with a mixture of frustration and sadness.

"It isn't a certain truth," she said quietly. I've met mages who aren't—" She hesitated, searching for the right words, "who aren't just...evil."

Aver's expression remained resolute, though a flicker of doubt crossed his face. "Even if there were one." He paused momentarily, "that still isn't enough to justify the atrocities of the others."

Leona's brow furrowed. "You're not giving magic—mages—much of a chance. Just because you may have seen some do horrible things doesn't mean all mages are the same."

Aver's gaze hardened again, and he shifted uncomfortably against the stone. "It's not just about seeing the worst. I've lived it. The damage, the calamity, the destruction. It's not something you forget."

Leona's voice softened, "I'm not asking you to forget everything you've seen. But would you blame the steel for the actions of a sword?" Leona's green eyes met Aver's, and the hardness in his gaze seemed to waver for a moment.

"And what if that sword turned its edge to the innocent? Would you still defend it?"

Leona shook her head slowly. "I'd make a shield from the steel."

Aver allowed a small smile to creep on his lips. He stared into the distance as if searching for something in the starlit night that could reassure him of his belief. Finally, he sighed, the tension in his shoulders easing.

"Maybe you're right," he said quietly, his voice almost uncertain. "Maybe there's a sliver of truth in what you're saying. Or maybe I just don't see an ounce of evil in you."

Leona's eyes widened for a moment as she began to blush.

She reached out to Aver, "Then let's make a promise. We'll look for the good together. Knights, mages," She met his eyes directly. "Let's find the good."

Aver glanced at her outstretched hand and then at her face, where a faint smile played at the corners of her lips. He hesitated and then clasped her hand slowly. "Alright. Let's try."

The moonlight bathed them in its gentle glow, and it almost felt comfortable for a moment.

As the moonlit night continued to illuminate the forest, Leona and Aver lost track of time. On the other side of those dense woods, Felle was frantically searching for any trace of the knight who had fled their battle.

His breath was heavy in his chest as he traversed the woods. The snapping of twigs and brush beneath his boots was the only sound in the eerie silence. The flames had all but chased away the remaining natural life. The moonlight shined down in silvery rays between the breaks in the trees. Felle could feel the exhaustion of using his awakened form during his battle with the knight.

He could not remember the last time he had allowed his cursed crown to adorn his head.

His long black hair was messy as it tousled around his lean shoulders. The slice on his cheek that the knight gave him had stopped its bleeding. The only trace that remained was the dried blood that stained his otherwise flawless face. His blue eyes were riddled with fatigue. He clenched his jaw. His thoughts were consumed with ghosts from the past, almost as though apparitions followed him. He could not escape the feeling that he was being haunted by a history long past.

He was certain the humans responsible for slaying the Fae were the very same who sought to snuff out the embers of magic among the humans, and yet, that human wielded a grimoire imbued with the magic of a long-dead boy. Not just any boy at that, but the very one that unraveled Vyes.

A thought crossed Felle's mind. His eyes filled with cold malice as the realization dawned on him. The Fae were never collateral damage, nor were they being senselessly slayed. They were a source of ammunition in a century-long power struggle.

His steps stalled; a deep, searing hatred burned within him. He watched through tear-stained eyes as so many were slaughtered. Near everything had been taken from him: his family, his people, and even his beliefs were shattered. The humans took away all that he held dear, and what has he gained? The Cursed Crown that adorns him when he fully awakens, and a single finite thread of Vyes. The only remaining thing in this world he deemed worthy of protecting. He pictured her innocent smile, large green eyes, and crimson hair from the day before. Leona was enough of a reason for him to put an end to this.

His steps began again, no longer stalled by the wounds he had burned deep within his soul. He would not allow her to be taken from him as well. She would not become but another blade to wield in a senseless war.

Felle had searched relentlessly through the woods. The soft glow of dusk was beginning to dance across the sky, and the soft light of morning was creeping lazily through the trees.

His blue eyes caught sight of the glimmer of water.

In the distance beyond the bend, the first rays of the sun illuminated a small pond and a small cave-like structure.

Leona was fast asleep against the entrance and inside lay a knight. Felle's eyes filled with cold intensity as he extended his hand and began to command the particles of light around him to form a dagger. The blade was illuminated in a soft golden glow, the edge sharp. He silently approached, his eyes unwavering and locked on the sleeping form of the knight. It was as though he was in a trance, seeing only the opportunity to kill. The knight's blond hair was a mess of dried blood and dirt against the cave's ground, his armor half removed, and a crude blood-soaked bandage wrapped around his muscular chest.

As he swiftly lifted the dagger above him, cold fingers grabbed his wrist. He turned to see Leona's tear-filled green eyes as she looked at him with terror.

In an instant, the blade began to flicker away in embers of golden light, and the tension in his wrist slowly eased under her touch.

"Please...don't," Leona's voice was barely a whisper.

Felle met her gaze. Her long, wild, crimson hair flowed around her like vines around a tree. Her dress was a mess of ash-stained tatters around her waif frame. Her emerald eyes were filled with tears that threatened to stain her pale cheeks at any moment. Her skin felt as cold as the dew that adorned the grass.

"I won't..." Felle's voice was soft as he uttered under his breath.

Gently, he pulled Leona to him. Thoughts evaded him as he buried his face in her hair and embraced her. Leona's eyes widened with shock, and after a moment, her arms embraced him back.

For the first time in a long time, a time so long Felle could not remember, he felt he wasn't too late.

Felle had broken away from his embrace with Leona. She quickly averted her eyes to the ground. "You found me," She breathlessly said.

"Was there ever a question I wouldn't?" Felle's voice was gentle as he addressed Leona.

Leona's eyes slowly trailed up to Felle's face until she landed on the dried blood upon his cheek. "You're hurt." Her brow furrowed as she examined him. His overcoat was singed from the flames, with cuts along the arms and torso.

"Is Dean okay?" Leona asked, worry clear in her tone. Felle's face pulled into a grimace as his annoyance clouded his features. He stepped back from Leona and leaned against a nearby tree.

"The idiot is fine." Felle averted his gaze as he crossed his arms. "The familiar and the others evacuated the town." Leona heaved a heavy sigh of relief. Felle gave Leona a thoughtful look; the rays of the sun cascaded on them, and he noticed the flickering reflection of light from the necklace around Leona's neck.

His eyes took on a seriousness. His long fingers gently inspected the vial bound to the chain. Cracks resounded around it; the liquid inside was half gone. He lifted his eyes to examine Leona closely. Her skin seemed to be paler than usual, and her nails appeared longer. His eyes widened with shock as he caught the slight inky black thorn pattern that now swirled at the tip of her shoulder, barely breaching the hem of the fabric of her dress.

His fingers reached to touch the mark as Leona flinched; his fingers hovered above her skin for a moment before he hesitantly pulled his hand back.

"You used magic again." His words were laced with seriousness, and his gaze was grim. Leona knew his words were not a question but an accusation.

"He was going to die..." she uttered, her eyes fixed on the forest floor as she tightly pinched the fabric of her dress between her fingers.

"How can you say this to me?" Felle's eyes were filled with betrayal as the emotion bled into his voice. "Are you determined to live the same cursed fate as her?" His hand gently tilted Leona's chin upwards to meet his gaze. Her eyes were filled with tears.

"Why would you risk your life for those who raise a hand against your own kind?" Felle's gaze was overwhelming; his presence was all-consuming.

Leona broke away from his touch and turned away from him.

"He saved me on the shoreline; how could I just let him bleed out? He isn't like the other knights, Felle; not all of them are-"

Felle's eyes clouded with anger. "Not like the others!" He let out a cold laugh. "We used to believe not all of them were alike, and then they slaughtered us. They are all the same." His voice was dripping with rage.

"I won't apologize for saving someone," Leona defiantly asserted. Felle approached Leona, sticking his face mere inches from hers,

"You may not know what they are, but I do, and as the keeper of The Isles, I have sworn my very blood to protect that which is of us." His anger was palpable, his voice unwavering. "It is time to lay these conflicts to rest. You will return with me to The Isles before you are consumed by your curse." Felle stepped away from Leona, her breath heavy in her chest. "I can't, Felle; I have to-." His eyes met hers once again,

"You gave me your word," his anger gave way to a quiet sadness. "Vyes-" he stopped himself too late. Leona looked at him with a mixture of confusion and hurt as it dawned on her that Felle saw only the reflection of her mother when he looked at her.

"I'm not her. I'll never be her." Leona's eyes pierced his as she straightened herself and walked back towards the small cave, where Aver still lay, sleeping.

18

Those Who Remained

The sun's golden rays bathed the freshly ashen cliffside. The breeze was heavy with a tinge of ash and smoke; the crumbling cobblestone shops and houses were all that remained of the sleepy seaside town. Dean slumped against the ruins of the Siren's Nest Tavern; his messy black hair gently caught the lingering breeze.

In his hand was the sword he had taken from Adira's cottage the day before in preparation for their upcoming journey back to Caillte, the same blade he used to hold back the kingdom's forces.

Dean's tired eyes searched the landscape in front of him. The townspeople had slowly shuffled back to the outskirts of Siren; the destruction the kingdom caused the people was horrific.

Adira hadn't returned since daybreak when she went to find Synth, Meldy, and Lyra.

Dean wondered if Leona was all right. He knew that she had escaped the knights, but he felt uneasy. Something about their encounter was off, especially the knight fighting Felle. He seemed too powerful. Dean knew that Felle was strong, and compared to the two knights they fought on the shore, the power difference was maddening.

"I bet Felle found her," the thought echoed in his mind. Dean hated the idea of Leona being alone and possibly hurt somewhere, but he also hated the idea of her being alone and vulnerable with Felle.

He couldn't help but picture her when she was no older than seven when they used to sneak out of the castle together. Leona always managed to find him, tears staining her tiny pink cheeks, terrified of either Yara or being shut away in her chambers by the palace servants. Mars was never far behind. Dean wondered if Mars had set out in search of Leona; he hadn't seen her since daybreak either.

Amongst the rubble, Dean caught sight of a small twinkle echoing the sun's rays; his fingers gently manipulated the ruins, and he pulled out a small trinket. He examined it, allowing the sun's rays to dance off it. The trinket appeared to be some kind of metal with an intricate design on it. Dean tucked it away in his pocket, making a note to ask Adira about it when she returned.

Dean found himself lost in thought again, thinking about Leona. His face deepened into a frown as he wondered where she was right now.

"Human boys really are gloomy," a lyrical voice echoed beside him. Dean was taken aback as he snapped his head to the left. His eyes caught sight of piercing red eyes and flowing blonde hair.

"What are you doing here?" Dean asked with a flustered annoyance. Meldy's small frame knelt beside him on the rubble near the tavern.

"We just came back from gathering the refugees." Her voice was pleasant, and her demeanor was bubbly. She smiled innocently.

Dean peered around the small woman, and Lyra and Synth stood a way back. As they approached, Dean noticed that there was someone behind them.

A tall knight with long white hair tangled with blood and ash, his red eyes unblinking as he followed closely behind Lyra; his armor was stained with blood, deep gouges had been torn through the metal, and ash encrusted nearly every surface.

"What the hell is going on?" Dean questioned them with a twisted confusion of suspicion and curiosity. Lyra met Dean's gaze and paused for a moment; she was hesitant to explain.

"He's harmless," she uttered through her teeth as she bit the inside of her cheek. Dean felt his face deepen into a scowl. "He tried to kill me mere hours ago!"

Lyra shifted uncomfortably and gave an awkward smile, "He's still bewitched, so he can't do anything I don't bid him to," she averted her gaze.

"You've gotta be kidding me," Dean uttered, annoyance present in his tone.

"Lyra would never do something to endanger the village," Synth interjected matter of fact and glared intently at Dean as though his objections were insults directed towards Lyra.

Dean pointed at the knight, "What happens when your magic runs out?" his eyes met hers.

"My magic won't run out!" Lyra was stricken. "I'm not some half-rate human mage! I'm a deity of the sea!" She protested back condescendingly.

Dean put his hand to his neck and began to sigh. "Where the

hell is Adira?" his gaze was full of impatience.

"She said she couldn't return now that her cover was blown and said to tell you to get out of town before they came back," Lyra stated plainly. Dean felt his jaw twist as he gritted his teeth. He couldn't believe Adira would run away after everything that happened.

The more he thought about it, the more he realized he didn't really know Adira that well; aside from stories he had heard about from Cyrus, he supposed she may be the type to disappear at a moment's notice.

The knight's dull red eyes gave Dean an uncomfortable chill. He scowled at Lyra. "Does he have to be so creepy?" Dean asked her through tired eyes.

"He has a name, you know?" Lyra remarked curtly.

"Does his name even matter?" Dean replied in protest.

"His name is Searel," Lyra interjected. Dean gave her an annoyed grimace. The knight before him was entirely terrifying, not for his strength but his dull eyes, sunken face, and zombie-like expression. His long white hair did little to improve the general pasty sheen on his skin, and upon closer inspection, Dean realized that this knight was the very same one who he had bumped into in that town outside the lost forest.

"I bumped into you that day!" Dean exclaimed to the knight; his expression remained stark and didn't seem to register Dean's words.

"He can't really hear you," Lyra uttered nervously while fumbling with her hands. "Once my spell takes effect, they are only able to see me and do as I will them." She shifted her gaze as she began to blush.

"Why don't you ask him to respond then?" Dean uttered,

annoyed.

Lyra gave Dean an incredulous look before turning her attention back to the knight. "Searel, you may speak." As soon as she had uttered the words, it was as though his dull eyes began to brighten ever so slightly, almost as if waking from a dream.

"Where is Aver?" his words were hoarse as they left his lips.

"Whose Aver?" Dean asked curiously,

"The blond knight that was on the shore." A look of realization washed over Dean, and then a look of panic as he realized that the last time he saw the man was while Leona was fleeing; could he have followed her?

"He is the Crown Prince of Aims." Searel's mild tone did little to calm Dean; he could feel the worry and anxiety beginning to boil inside him. The Crown Prince of the human kingdom was nowhere to be found, and neither was Leona, the only heir to Caillte. She was lost somewhere by herself or, worse, with him.

"If he's the crown prince, then why the hell were the knights trying to kill him!" Dean erupted at Searel, his black hair wildly cascading around his face.

"They are the king's guard, but they do not serve the king nor the realm," Searel replied, his red eyes and emotionless face giving nothing away.

Dean approached the knight and met his gaze directly,

"What the hell do you mean they don't serve the king or the realm?" Dean's expression was one of a twisted intensity. Searel met his gaze, remaining expressionless. "They service the High Order of Aims." A quizzical look crossed Dean's face. He had never heard of the High Order. Neither Adira nor Felle uttered a word about it to him.

Synth and Meldy gave Dean a nervous glance as they quietly retreated to the upper part of the hill. Lyra avoided Dean's gaze.

"What do you know?" Dean questioned her as he turned his attention to the pink-haired woman.

"N-nothing," she mumbled, averting her gaze as she fumbled with her fingers. Dean's blue eyes narrowed as he approached her. He was quite a bit taller than Lyra; her small form looked up at him.

"We should really get going-" she uttered.

"What is the High Order?" Dean asked her once again. His tone was not severe, but his eyes were as he again questioned her. Lyra hesitated before meeting his gaze once again; her face was painted with a look of uncomfortable annoyance.

"The High Order declared the first war against mages..." she quietly uttered. "They disappeared into obscurity seventeen years ago after the armistice between the magic and non-magic realms was formed." Dean was taken aback. He had never heard of this history in Caillte. He knew of the law binding those to the forest and that it was forbidden to leave to the human realm, but he never knew that there was a war that had plagued the nation or that there was a ceasefire that occurred seventeen years prior.

"What does she mean there was a cease-fire?" Dean questioned him.

"Seventeen years ago, Rowan of the king's guard wed a political emissary named Melia from the foreign Kingdom of Ashvaha across the seas to strengthen the relationship between nations. She disappeared a year after she married him and was thought to have been slain by the mages of the lost forest in retaliation for the previous war the High Order declared." Searel spoke flatly.

"The crazy guy with the black hair who set this place ablaze? His wife?" Dean was taken aback but tried to maintain his questioning.

"Rowan became increasingly cruel and cold after Melia had disappeared. Truly bitter, a man hollowed by loss, his patience and tolerance wore thin as each year passed without her. She was believed to have been with child."

"None of the mages in Caillte would have ever done this," Dean said in disbelief. "They aren't evil..." he uttered.

"You know not a thing you speak of, human boy; the truth is much grayer than you can even perceive," Lyra spoke crossly.

"So everyone's just been lying this whole time?" Dean questioned with anger in his voice. His blue eyes ablaze with a silent fury.

"I know not what the humans have told you, nor do I align with their choices in doing so. The deities of the Sea and the Fae do not concern themselves with the human's affairs." Lyra spoke calmly; however, her demeanor betrayed her voice. Her shoulders were tense, and her face was pulled into a grimace with a hint of disgust.

Dean glared at her. "You seem to like that human enough to concern him with your affairs." Dean pointed his slender finger at Searel, who wore the same dead-eyed expression as earlier.

Lyra stomped her foot at Dean's accusation; her face had turned a shade of pink, slightly darker than her hair.

"You don't know anything! You're just a dumb human, so I don't care what you think." She crossed her arms defiantly and looked at Dean through glared eyes.

Dean rolled his eyes, "I don't have time for this; I need to find Leona." Dean started toward the edge of the hill where Synth and Meldy had previously retreated.

He looked over his shoulder from atop the hill.

"If you see Adira, tell her to go to Caillte," Dean uttered intensely.

Dean was sure that whether Adira received his message or not, she was unlikely to come. He could not think about the what-ifs right now; however, his thoughts about Leona and the uncertainty surrounding her were to be prioritized above all else. Dean's boots were heavy as they crushed the brush and ash beneath him.

Who was he kidding? Whether he found her or not, he was not capable of shielding her from what may lie ahead; the kingdom's strength was a grim reminder of how much weaker Dean was than he realized, for all the thoughts that consumed him of his inferiority, the blaring one remained. Felle was stronger, and he was probably already with her. Dean clenched his fist as he continued to search through the brush. Anger and resigned defeat burrowed heavily in his chest.

"Cyrus, Yara, and even Sir Mikail were right...I'm not worthy to stand by her side." Anger coiled in Dean's chest, but he swallowed it, its bitter taste lingering like ash in his mouth as he contended with his inferiority. As he continued each step through the brush and ash-encrusted dirt of the nearby forest, he could not help but remember the many memories of his time growing up in Caillte.

The memories were as clear as day to him now, the many late nights under the stars after spending the day training relentlessly. He would look up at the vast sky, and all his thoughts would fall on who he would become as a knight. More than anything, Dean desired the power to protect that which he held dear, and she took the form of a crimson-haired girl with green eyes more vibrant than any forest.

He remembered the many instructions the head of the

knights, Sir Mikail, had given him to pursue this path; he could smell the morning dew when he would train with him and the other knights. He could still feel the soft grain of the leather of his gloves or the way it felt when Sir Mikail adjusted his stance. He recalled each correction to carefully and tirelessly hone his swordsmanship.

Dean remembered the daily strain to grow stronger, to shed the skin of an abandoned boy, and to become a knight worthy of protecting the forest and the mages. This trial he took on willingly, but in truth, all of it—the countless hours and endless corrections—had always been for her.

The physical strain day in and day out to mold himself into someone worthy of bearing the responsibility of her well-being was a weight he did not realize he was not yet strong enough to bear.

Dean stopped, his gaze drifting over the dense woods. He clenched his fist, driving it hard into the bark of a nearby tree. The rough surface scraped his knuckles, grounding him; the tension within momentarily appeased.

The briefly appeased tension simmered within him as he moved through the forest, each step breaking brush and earth beneath him. Memories of his sacrifices to bear the kingdom's crest echoed through his mind, keeping time with the steady beat of his footsteps.

"Had Cyrus not given him a home? A purpose? A father in Sir Mikail?" The weight of Dean's guilt pressed down, thick and unyielding. He'd let Leona end up in danger, failed to protect her, and in doing so, betrayed Cyrus—the man who had given him everything to make her safety his purpose. How could he face either of them now?

He clenched his fists, and his steps took on a new urgency.

This would not be the end. He would find her, grow stronger in doing so, and protect her—even if it cost him his life. Felle might be stronger, better equipped to keep her safe, but Dean refused to falter now. Better or worse, he would stay by her side, no matter the pain or sacrifice. Leona was the only person who felt like home, and even if it meant sacrificing a future with her, he would give everything to protect that.

19

The Forbidden Lands

The sun shone brightly in the sky, and the smell of smoke was steadily drifting away with the winds. Aver sat cross-legged, his messy blond hair falling in gentle tousles on his face. A look of annoyance was present on his face, and his arms were folded to his chest tightly.

"I know I promised, but-" Aver hesitated for a moment, "come on." Aver looked at Leona incredulously on the other side of the small cave. She averted his eyes as she gathered her legs to her chest. Felle leaned against the cave entrance; his long black hair fell perfectly around him. His eyes were shut as he pinched the bridge of his nose as if seeing the scene around him would cause him pain.

"Shut up, human," Felle uttered condescendingly. Aver clenched his jaw as he turned his attention to Felle.

"No one asked you, demon," Aver growled back. Felle's eyes opened into a glare as he gazed at the knight; his makeshift bandage was stained with dried blood as it clung to his muscular frame. A cruel smile pulled at Felle's lips,

"If only those wounds had been left undone, you'd be long dead by now." Felle wore a smug smirk as he observed Aver's tense demeanor.

"Stop it." Leona startled them as she spoke; she had been quiet for so long that they had forgotten her presence for a moment.

Felle's blue eyes gazed at Leona, who quickly averted her gaze in avoidance. Felle's face immediately pulled into a scowl. "You cannot be angry with me forever—" Felle began, his words trailing off as Leona's eyes met his. She hadn't uttered a word in response, but Felle could see the anger behind her eyes.

"If you're going to have a lovers' quarrel, can you take it over there?" Aver said with annoyance clear in his tone. Leona's green eyes widened in shock, which soon gave way to embarrassment. Her cheeks began to turn pink.

"It's not like that!" she exclaimed. Still averting her eyes from Felle. Aver's eyes softened as he looked upon Leona.

"I have to return to Aims." Aver's voice was soft as he spoke to Leona.

"Aren't the king's guard trying to kill you?" Leona asked with worry in her voice. Aver paused momentarily as he pulled himself up,

"Rowan and his band of fools aren't brave enough to raise a hand to me in the kingdom's presence." He spoke matter of fact as he slowly pulled his armor back on, "I'm sure they've already reported to my father that you and those mages slaughtered me." A smirk pulled at his lips, "Guess I'll have to haunt the castle until I get him alone and put an end to him." he laughed softly.

"Are you sure you'll be alright?" Leona questioned him

gently. She approached him, and her eyes fell upon the gauze that bandaged his chest beneath the armor. He met her eyes,

"I'll be fine." He smiled brightly at Leona. His eyes looked behind her, and he glared intensely. He quickly pulled his face into a frown. "Die," he uttered at Felle as he straightened himself and affixed his sword around his waist again.

Aver cast his eyes to the sky as though he were reading the sun itself; after a few moments, he set off towards the edge of the clearing.

"Wait! You don't have a map!" Leona hurried after him. Aver looked at her over his shoulder,

"No need; I can read the direction of the sun. I know where I'm going." Leona gave him a bewildered look before nodding. "Stay out of trouble." He smirked before disappearing into the forest.

Leona felt a new resolve burning within her. Aver was strong, and she was certain he would clear the mage's names, at least for what happened in Siren. Her red hair tousled around her in wild waves. Her green eyes caught Felle's gaze from the corner of her vision. He quickly averted his gaze.

"I won't go to The Isles," Leona said calmly; Felle grimaced before meeting her gaze. "You promised me," he said, his eyes intense.

"I'm not done breaking my curse," Leona protested. Felle let out an exasperated sigh. "You can't break it; you have no idea what you are doing, let alone how much damage you are causing to yourself," He argued. Leona stood firm, her face unshifted by his protests.

"This is a senseless endeavor," Felle spoke as if commanding the words to be true. Leona did not back down, "

I'm going back to Caillte. To face my father...to face the truth." Her words were not sharp. However, they still pierced Felle.

"The false king can't break your curse; I've already told-" Leona cut Felle's words off, "I don't care what you've told me; I'm going back to Caillte." Her green eyes were ablaze with conviction. "I'm not going to run anymore." Felle was at a loss for words. Leona had done many things that he could not understand, but he felt this defined all logic.

"You'll die of your curse," Felle began.

"I refuse to die from my curse," Leona corrected him.

A shuffling in the brush took them off guard; they frantically surveyed their surroundings before Leona's eyes stopped on the brush at the edge of the clearing, where a black tail coiled behind the leaves.

"Mars!" Leona shouted as she ran to her. In the blink of an eye, Leona was on the forest floor with tears streaming down her face as she embraced the black cat in her arms. Mars straightened herself after a moment before peering into Leona's eyes.

"Let's go home, Leona," Mars spoke softly. Leona's tear-filled eyes widened in shock. "I can hear you!" she gasped.

"Hello, familiar," Felle uttered under his breath. Mars straightened herself once again and approached Felle.

"We're going back to Caillte Felle," Mars softly asserted to him. Felle peered at her; after a moment of regarding her in silence, he let out a defeated sigh. "I won't stand in the way of your promise," He spoke softly to Mars. She looked at him with her wide green eyes,

"Please keep your promise to me as well," Mars gently reminded him. A sad smile pulled at Felle's lips. Leona looked between them questioningly, sure that she remembered Mars not liking Felle. What promise could they have made?

Leona gathered all the courage she had remaining in her as she approached Felle. His blue eyes met hers, and with sad resignation, he parted his lips ever so slightly.

"I'm sorry, Leona." His words were barely a whisper, and as he uttered the apology, he averted his gaze.

Leona was surprised; this was the first time Felle had used her name. She extended her hand to him, smiling softly, "Let's go to Caillte." Felle met her gaze again with a surprised expression. A small smile pulled at Felle's lips; he clasped her outstretched hand.

He looked over his shoulder at the dense line of trees before calling out. "Come on, idiot; we're going to Caillte." Leona gave Felle a confused look just as Dean emerged from the brush. His messy black hair gently blew with the breeze, revealing his vibrant blue eyes. Dean was clad in his fitted black tunic, pants, and boots. A sword fixed to his hip and a severe look on his face. Leona broke away from Felle and ran to him, throwing herself in his arms as she hugged him tightly.

"Dean!" she breathed as tears rolled down her cheeks. Dean held onto Leona as he steadied her in his arms.

"I'm so glad you're okay," he uttered softly before pulling her away from him and examining her with a serious look on his face. Leona began to laugh.

"I'm fine!" She exclaimed. Dean's eyes hovered over the thorny curse mark swirling up her shoulder to her neck. The inky black reminder of their time running out. Leona stiffened her lip and met his eyes. "Let's end this." Dean gave her a wry smile; worry clouded his eyes.

"Okay, let's go." Dean walked with Leona next to him to the center of the clearing, where Felle stood with Mars next to his feet.

Felle gave Leona one last look before snapping his fingers. In a split second, the clearing erupted in light. Tendrils of soft white reached up, forming a barrier around them. The wind stilled completely; Felle straightened and spoke commandingly,

"As Keeper of The Isles, I bid thee to my will." The light began to take on a dark hue, as if black was nipping at the edge of the white light. Felle's face was one of stoic determination as a twisted mark began to etch itself into his skin. The mark took on the form of inky black thorns, twisting into a Crown upon his forehead. His blue eyes met Leona's. Her breath caught in her chest; Felle was more powerful than she would have even imagined. His black hair cascaded around him as he continued to bid his magic to obey him. He outstretched his hand, "Unbind the trees and the winds, and deliver me to the lost forest of Caillte." Upon the command, the light completely enveloped them.

20

Home Is Where The Truth Lies

As dusk approached, the sun was beginning to set. The magnificent spiraling towers of the Kingdom of Aims were a sight to
behold as the last of the sun danced off the white stone.

Aver approached slowly as he quietly slipped into the stables
outside of the castle. Against the wooden side of the stables was
a set of cloaks left by the knights on watch. He quietly pulled
one over himself and disappeared through the corridor to the
castle annex. Aver's steps were light as he carefully made his
way through the inner parts of the castle. Usually, it would be a
bustle with servants and guards by this time. Something was
off. Aver craned his head to see past the rounding corner. There
was no one.

He quietly continued down the hall; the sound of a door
opening startled him as he tucked himself out of sight against a
groove along the hall. In the corner of his eye, he saw a woman
he had never seen before; her dark hair and brown eyes were

twisted into a serious expression. She was carrying a small lantern in her hand, her body shrouded in a servant's cloak. Aver silently followed behind her a way back to keep out of sight; as he followed, he noticed she was winding further into the castle.

Her footsteps stalled as Aver tucked himself behind the wall that turned the corner; afraid he had been found out, he silently braced himself.

After a few moments of silence, he again peered around the corner. However, the woman was nowhere to be seen.

Before him, down the long hall, was a small opening protruding from the wall itself. Aver's eyes widened as he realized what he was looking at. He approached quickly and pulled the area of the protruding wall. It gave way under his touch, revealing a hidden passage and winding stairs to go down. Aver felt a pit in his stomach.

He took one final glance over his shoulder at the long corridor's innermost interior before disappearing into the darkness and down the winding steps.

Aver's eyes quickly adjusted to the darkness that surrounded him as he transversed down the long, winding steps. He had never been here before; he had never even heard anyone mention a secret corridor within the castle. His eyes caught the flickering light of a soft glow at the bottom of the steps; Aver slowed his pace. As he reached the final step, he turned his head.

There was a narrow stone hallway with a torch lining the walls. He looked to his left and then his right, unsure of which direction to take first. He craned his ears to try and detect any sound, and as if hearing a pin drop, he heard what sounded like the clanking of armor in the distance down the left hall.

Aver quietly approached, careful to keep himself against the side of the wall and obscure himself from any prying eyes.

Before his eyes could adjust, he heard Rowan's unmistakable voice in the distance. Aver clenched his jaw as he reached for his sword that was holstered at his waist. Silently approaching and rounding the corner, his eyes widened as he knelt and peered over the edge of the corner.

Cells lined the damp walls of this place. It was as though a secret dungeon was forged beneath the castle. Aver's golden eyes caught the form of Rowan from the side of his vision; Auden and Mercer were along with him.

Aver was more on edge, knowing the entire king's guard was present in this secret place. The sound of a piercing scream washed terror over him. He stayed frozen in place as his eyes adjusted to the scene before him.

Rowan dragged a man bound by chains behind him against the damp, jagged stones that lined this dungeon. He heard the murmurs of voices echoing from the cells.

Rowan dragged the man to a large stone table before throwing his frail and broken body against it. Aver was full of disgust and shock at what he was observing.

Rowan pulled out a few blades from his sheath and flung them against the man's skin, piercing him as another pained scream erupted from him. Blood poured along the grooves of the stone table.

"You had one task, demon," Rowan sneered at the man who lay broken on the table. "All I asked was for something I could use to crumble that damned treaty," Rowan tossed a tattered book on the table, splattering blood with a thud. "Fail again, and I will tear you limb from limb," Rowan threatened coldly as a cruel smile pulled at his lips. He grabbed the chain that bound the man and forced him forward where the blood-soaked pages of the tattered book lay.

The man slowly made his way to the book, gently touching it. Rowan twisted the blade that protruded from his frail back as he let out another tortured scream with tears streaming down his face.

"I'm waiting," Rowan jeered. Auden averted his eyes while Mercer watched on with a twisted excitement. The man began to emanate light from his hands as it flowed into the book. Aver could not believe what he was seeing; he was certain that this was magic, but why would the king's guard, charged with protecting the kingdom and hunting the mages, use one like this?

After a moment, the man collapsed against the table as the light flickered out. Rowan quickly collected the book and handed it to Mercer. He grabbed the chain and threw the man against the stone floor. Mercer approached the far wall and touched the book to it; in an instant, a new door formed out of flecks of golden light. The door fell away like sand, and they deposited themselves inside. Aver forced himself up and quietly followed after them.

He silently snuck in behind them to reveal books lining the walls; the tomes were all different sizes and shapes.

Aver ducked under a row and continued out of sight; he watched intently from the sides, hidden from view, as Rowan placed the new book into a small slat on the wall.

Aver peered around the corner to observe Rowan and his men. They were sorting through the tomes on the far wall,

"Did you find it?" Rowan barked at Mercer impatiently. Mercer handed him a large tome from the wall without a second word. A wicked smile pulled at Rowan's lips as he motioned for them to follow. Auden retrieved a different tome from one of the walls. "This one?" he said, holding the book for Rowan to see.

"That one should work." They set out through the door, and as soon as they stepped over the threshold, particles began to materialize, sealing it behind Aver.

Aver stayed tucked out of sight until he could no longer hear their footsteps. He breathed a heavy sigh of relief as he pulled his hood down with a furrowed brow.

He quickly rose to his feet and began investigating the strange library. He began to explore the book-lined walls; the books appeared to have a magnetism to them. As he saw the other book, Aver wondered if they were all imbued with magic. Aver had never seen such a place before. A forbidden library below the kingdom? Not just any library but one that was filled with magic, the cardinal sin of the Kingdom of Aims.

Aver began to shuffle through some of the books; stacks of parchments and letters were neatly collected in cubbies along the back wall. He was in awe.

The room was a magnificent and large library, larger than even the kingdom's scholar library. Shelves lined every wall, rows upon rows intertwined through the library halls, and books riddled every surface.

As he walked, he skimmed the many tomes; he stopped at the area Rowan was in and noticed the book they just had was tucked away on the shelf. He gently pulled it out, and blood dripped from the pages. There could be no mistake; this was the book he had just witnessed them imbue with magic. Aver quickly slipped it back into its spot before striding up the stairs of the library. He noticed a small table at the end of another long corridor.

He paused for a moment as he saw pieces of parchment stacked messily against it. His fingers gently manipulated the stack as he pulled forth the parchment. His eyes widened as he realized what he was looking at.

This parchment was no ordinary sheet of paper. It was a map of the nation. Aver examined it closely, and this map was not the same one that he had seen hanging in the castle, nor was it accurate. It revealed the lost forest outside of the town of Tearn to the west; the forest had another kingdom marked on it, *Caillte*; it was written in a script Aver was not familiar with; he deduced it must be a mage script. His gaze continued intently, examining the map. Tearn was a day trip to the kingdom, and his finger ran along the roads and paths from Tearn to Deorad. The forest he had encountered Leona was between the mountainside and Siren, which was marked as forbidden lands. As he continued studying it, he saw a cove marked near Siren in another unfamiliar script. The seas were marked, and a small island was indicated across the vast expanse of ocean, the script also unknown to Aver.

The map revealed known regions that the kingdom had taken out and hidden; the surrounding nations and countries were the same outside of the regions, yet, in the kingdom, the discrepancies were evident. There was no date listed. However, Aver knew better. This map was the real map of the realm.

He wondered if the forbidden regions were where those prisoners were from or if they were from the lost woods of Caillte. What more was the kingdom hiding? Aver knew his father had to know. There was not a scenario in which he didn't.

If Rowan gets his hands on Leona, will they inflict the same fate upon her as a cursed being? Aver pushed the thought from his mind.

Running his finger across the Kingdom of Aims to Tearn and past that. Aver parted his lips as he continued to trace along the map, running his finger to Deorad. Next to it, the cliffside of Siren. Past that, across the sea, the island he noticed earlier was marked with that strange writing; below it was a small translation. Aver's eyes widened as he read the words *The Gate of Eternity*.

The crinkled edge of the parchment map had little tatters down the side; Aver gently rolled it into a scroll before placing it into the inner part of his armored chest. He gently sifted through the piles of parchment and loose pages on the small table.

Pages upon pages were riddled with strange writing and attempted translations. Among the papers, Aver discovered old letters; after peering at them for a moment, he realized they were records of the first war.

He began to read the letter. They spoke of a tribe of human-like beings impervious to age, illness, and affliction. They were described as beautiful and were given names throughout the century that inspired stories: demons, elves, fairies, and others. They most closely related themselves to the term Fae; they were a race that readily possessed magic; it was within them, unlike humans. A century before, the Kingdom of Aims was in a bitter war with the prevailing Kingdom of the Lost Forest of Caillte in a power struggle. The Kingdom of Caillte had obtained the ability to use magic by means of magic-imbued books known as grimoires that had been given to them centuries before by the Fae in an act of diplomacy between the races. The Knights of the Kingdom of Aims began hunting and capturing members of the Fae to obtain magic to turn the war in their favor against Caillte.

The war resulted in the two kingdoms effectively closing themselves off from the other's realm seventeen years prior after an unfathomable loss from the Kingdom of Aims shook the realm, shattering a political alliance with the foreign Kingdom of Ashvaha across the seas. They had sent a political emissary who was betrothed to the highest-ranking knight of the kingdom. At the height of the war, she disappeared without a trace and was believed to have been slain by the mages of the forest.

The treaty separated the human realm from those who implored the use of magic and stated that humans were not to transverse the Lost Forest of Caillte or interact with its magic-using dwellers. In turn, the mages that resided in the forest were never to venture into the human realm or interact with the non-magic-using realms. Magic was strictly forbidden beyond the walls of the forest that enclosed Caillte.

Aver turned over the other pages; as he continued to read, he noticed a grouping of pages towards the back of the pile. He pulled them forward. They appeared to be translations from loose pages of mage script that were fastened behind each page.

Twenty years before, a mage and his sister sought the help of old allies that had been handed down through the centuries. In their journey to find the Fae, they encountered Aims knights who attempted to dispose of them. The siblings were separated in the forbidden realm forest, and the brother was mortally wounded and left to die near a clearing.

A crimson-haired being with green eyes encountered him in the forest and offered him aid; he thought she was an angel; the moment she laid eyes on him, it was as though she could see his very soul. She treated his wounds and left him to rest; the man remained delirious; days gave way to nights in those woods, and by the light of the morning, he could feel his life force fading;

she had returned to his side once again; she bore a jeweled dagger, and the wind around her began to whip. Golden light emanated from the blade; she began to speak; her voice was smooth and soft. "With this blade, I sever the bonds of this realm, come forth the thread of destiny, and weave together a new path;" the man's body began to emanate the same light, a red thread weaved its way around his wrist, in tandem with the woman. As the light began to settle, he could feel his wounds begin to close, inky black marks twisted around the woman, a choker-like collar burned into the soft white skin of her throat, her wrist and ankles bore the same vine-like form, as though she wore chains of thorns themselves. His wounds began to seal, death fell away from him, and a renewed resolve washed over him.

The sister who had tirelessly searched the woods for him was injured and messy, but she was elated to see that her brother had not succumbed. She helped him to his feet, and the woman of the forbidden forest returned with them to the kingdom.

Aver paused for a moment as his fingers grazed the edge of leather amongst the piles of parchment. He fished out a small leather book tied with string. The brown book had strange writing etched into the side and was tied completely shut; he slowly pulled the knot at the front until it fell away, revealing a journal of sorts. He began thumbing through the pages until he reached the middle, where multiple pieces of tattered parchment were held; they appeared to be more translations.

Finding the people of the forbidden lands and forest would be a long journey. With the threat of war ever looming, my brother and I set out to seek their aid in the hope they would help the people of Caillte as they had one hundred years before. Today is the day we cross the threshold of the lost forest and seek our destiny...

Aver's brow furrowed as he read the words. The armistice has been in effect for the last seventeen years. Could this be from before that? He turned to the next page; another translation awaited him.

The humans in the villages are nothing like we were told. They helped my brother and me find the town outside of the Forbidden Forest. Brother thinks we should be cautious, but they have been so kind to us....

Aver could feel unease settle within him as he turned the next page. Dried blood soaked the borders of the parchment.

I'm so sorry...I was so wrong. The humans tricked us and attacked brother. We ran into the forest and got separated. He was bleeding so much...

Aver turned the blood-soaked pages until he found another translation amongst them.

Providence or fate has smiled down upon us. Brother and I returned home to the Lost Forest of Caillte.

I was certain he had been ripped from this plain until I found him days later, in a small clearing in the Forbidden Forest; his wounds were healed, and a beautiful being tended to him. Her hair was the color of the most vivacious roses, and her eyes were as green as the forest. She had pointed ears and a delicate constitution.

Around her wrists and ankles were black marks that looked like the thorny stems of roses that twisted like bracelets; her neck bore the same mark, almost like a choker. Her voice was soft, and she returned with us to Caillte...

Aver's eyes widened in shock as he turned the page, and a small portrait was inlaid in the journal. The woman they described with crimson hair and green eyes bore an uncanny resemblance to Leona if it weren't for her mature face and pointed ears. The silver-haired man and woman who stood beside her also looked oddly familiar. Where had he seen her before, he wondered; her freckled face flashed in his mind.

Aver turned his attention back to the portrait and studied it intently; the woman in the photo looked almost exactly like Leona, except for a few subtle differences between them and the curse mark Leona had. This woman had marks, but were they that of a curse, too?

Aver's breath was heavy in his chest as he shuffled through the pages once more. He saw a name etched into the leather of the book in the same strange script, along with a crest. As he continued flipping through, he realized this was translated into the other letters of records to fit the language of the kingdom.

The journal must have belonged to someone from the royal family of Caillte. There was no reason for Aims to have this. Aver continued to examine the journal; however, there were no more translations. He quickly gathered the pages back, along with the letters of record, and bound them within the book before tying it tightly and tucking it away in his chest plate.

Aver looked around the library once more. There was a sort of magnetism in the air of this place; he thought it was entirely strange and unnerving. He wound back down the stairs and followed the long hall lined with books back to where the door had materialized. In a matter of seconds, the door had begun to dissolve into particles before him. He walked through it and back into the dismal dungeons that smelled of rot. He gave an empathetic look to the cells full of what he now presumed to be Fae.

Aver's eyes scanned the room, and his breath caught in his throat as he realized the depths of depravity he was seeing. Beneath the castle in this hidden space were not just small cells, but each housed human-like beings with pointed ears and otherworldly characteristics. Not unlike the woman in the portrait inside the journal. Unlike the woman in the portrait, these beings were filthy, tortured, and bloodied.

He turned his attention to the bloodied man who collapsed on the stone floor. His red hair was coated in dirt and dried blood, and his pointed ears were an indication of his lineage. Aver felt a chill run down his being as the weight of what they were doing here heavily pulled at him. The king's guard was still using these creatures to harvest magic for a war that was supposed to be long over. Unease settled within his bones; he remembered Rowan's remark about ending the treaty to that man on the floor. Was Rowan trying to fan the flames of war again? The letters of record mentioned the cause of the ceasefire as the loss of that political emissary who was betrothed to the highest-ranking knight. Could that have been Rowan?

Aver felt his unease begin to eat away at him. He needed to find his father.

Aver quietly maneuvered about the castle after leaving the hidden dungeon below. As he investigated, he found that the castle was still quiet and devoid of personnel. From the corner of his eye, he caught the end of flowing blond hair and satin gowns.

He turned to see his mother and little sister walking the long corridor to their chambers. He gave a cautious look around before following after them. His mother's flowing blonde hair and demure appearance were precisely how you would imagine the queen of a kingdom; her golden eyes and fair skin were elegantly complemented by the many ornate jewels that encrusted her gown and the golden tiara that sat atop her head, held up by perfect posture and a regal demeanor.

Aver's mother was not quite forty, though she had the mannerisms of a mature monarch. Next to her was his little sister, a nearly identical copy of their mother, with her blonde hair and violet eyes, the perfect representation of the attributes of both their parents. His sister wore an equally impressive gown encrusted with gems and ornate detailing; even though she was merely fifteen, she was every bit as proper and primed as you would expect the crown princess to be.

"Mother, is what Father said true?" her quiet voice echoed throughout the corridor.

They slowed their steps as she turned to meet her daughter's gaze. A gentle hand lay against her fair skin, "Cassia, it is not your place to concern yourself with matters of the kingdom. Your Father will return once he completes his work." her voice was smooth yet firm.

"What about brother? Is it true that he was slain?" her voice shook as tears threatened to fall from her eyes. Their mother carefully wiped the tears from her large violet eyes where they had pooled,

"I am certain Aver will return, just as I am certain your Father will." her voice softened as she comforted Cassia. She straightened her posture and began her strides once again with Cassia in tow.

Aver had stilled himself behind one of the pillars that lined the corridors of the inner castle to remain hidden from view. A feeling of despair began to twist inside of him; he wondered if Rowan was responsible for his father's absence. He clenched his fist at the realization that he was going to be leaving both his mother and little sister there without a word; he felt guilty, considering that they seemed to wonder if he was even alive. He knew he could not stay in the castle and wait for whatever calamity Rowan handed down.

He slipped past the corridors and stopped in front of the large doors that enclosed the throne room; Aver's eyes quickly scanned the room as he made his way inside. It was empty; the only trace of life was a declaration pinned to the board near the war room. Aver pulled it down and quickly stowed it along with what he had gathered from the dungeon below before slipping outside the castle and making his way into the town outside the kingdom and towards the road that led to Tearn.

He knew one person who desired peace in the kingdom as much as he did and knew she was never far from where the mages were. Armed with what he had discovered in the hidden dungeon, he set out to find an ally in the form of a cursed woman who bore an uncanny resemblance to a member of the royal family of the mages' forest.

21

The Lost Forest Kingdom

Bright light erupted, blaring and obscuring everything around it. Luminous and daunting, the power that surged around the trees and brush was all-consuming and fleeting. The light slowly resided like water from a shoreline; in the middle of the circle, Felle stood Leona, Mars, and Dean beside him.

The sun had all but given way to night. Leona turned her eyes to the tree line, and a wave of familiarity washed over her. They were within the forest walls of Caillte. She was home. Felle grasped Leona's wrist as she set off,

"Do as you must." He met her gaze intensely, "And I will do as I must," he uttered sternly. Leona felt fear begin to rise in her chest. Felle allowed his hand to fall from Leona's wrist as he averted his eyes. The black crown of thorns slowly flecked away from his pale skin. Mars peered up at Leona from her feet where she had wrapped herself, "Let's go, Leona!" she cooed. Dean silently walked behind them; his messy black hair covered his eyes.

Leona was certain that he was feeling the weight of the impending consequences of their actions. Every step took them deeper into the forest and closer to the very thing she feared most. Confronting the past that has led to the present she is no longer running from. Her hair whipped wildly around her as she broke into a sprint towards the castle.

The memories of her father flashed into her mind through the years. She knew there was no going back. Her eyes filled with tears as the moss-covered stone came into view. The castle she spent years longing to run from was before her again.

Instantaneously, she heard the clanking of metal from the trees around them. Leona whipped her head around as she saw the knights of Caillte surround them with swords drawn. At the helm was the unmistakable form of Sir Mikail, the head of the Caillte knights. His straw-colored hair and usual kind eyes were obscured by a cold resolve and the metal of his helmet. Leona was painfully aware that they had returned traitors.

"Stop! What are you doing!" She screamed at the knights. One of the knights approached Dean with his sword drawn and forced him to bend his knee as he held the steel of the blade against his throat. Dean clenched his jaw and looked onward. He had no desire to fight the other knights; they had raised him and taught him how to fight and what it meant to carry the crest of the kingdom. A flash rang out as inky black tendrils propelled the blade away from Dean's throat. Felle's voice was stark,

"Stand, boy. This will not be your execution." He approached Dean as the knights began to charge them. Dean drew his sword and took his stance next to Felle with his resolve strengthened. As much as he did not desire to fight the men he considered his brothers in arms, he had something more precious than those bonds, and saving Leona was all-consuming to him. Sir Mikail wasted no time striking Dean's sword with all his might; Dean tilted his blade quickly before countering and forcing him back.

Each blow a thunderous clash; Dean's swordsmanship was ever improving and adapting, and Sir Mikail had praised him for and carefully honed the very skills that were now turned against him.

"You swore an oath," Sir Mikail spat the words as they clashed.

"I kept my oath." Dean's eyes were marred with an unbreakable resolve. The sound of the metal clashing and the tension in the air was suffocating; Leona was at a loss as Dean continued to take on the head of the knights of Caillte.

"You betrayed your brothers," Sir Mikail spoke venomously as he pulled forth a second sword, narrowly missing Dean's throat. Leona watched as they clashed, a flurry of sparks and accusations.

"I honored my promise," Dean coldly declared as he gained the upper hand. Sir Mikail's face grew tense as he observed the battle turning; he gave the other knights the order to attack.

Leona let out a scream as she reached for them.

A resounding boom rang out, and a heavy force pushed them back. Felle continued striding ahead towards the castle's gate, unfazed.

The other knights were temporarily stunned and on the dirt; Felle did not kill them, nor did he lessen the force with which he removed them from his path. He glanced at Dean, noticing he was unharmed, before continuing forward.

"How dare you step within the bounds of my forest." A cold voice commanded from the gate. Leona felt shock wring throughout her body as her eyes found the source of the voice.

His towering frame, silver hair, and gray eyes were ablaze with a cold fury; his regal white robes began to lift slightly around him as blades of wind formed and thrashed around him. "Father," Leona uttered her voice barely a whisper. He turned his gaze to Leona; her small frame felt an unimaginable weight as he looked upon her.

"Where the hell have you been?" he growled at Leona.

"I–" the words would not leave her lips. Cyrus's steely eyes peered down at Leona from the gates; she had never felt so small.

Felle continued his stride, his long hair billowing behind him as the twilight light descended. Particles of light began to form in his hand; at the edges, sparks of black lightning licked at the blade.

"Now, is that any way to speak to someone you cherish?" Felle sneered at Cyrus. Cyrus's tense demeanor stiffened as if striking a nerve, and he pulled forth a sword.

Cyrus's grip on the hilt of his sword tightened, the blade gleaming ominously in the dim light. The air around him seemed to vibrate with an ancient power, as if the weapon itself was alive, reacting to the fury in his heart. Leona's breath caught in her throat—she had heard whispers of this blade, a weapon forged in a time long forgotten, one that her father had sworn never to wield again.

"Cyrus," Felle's voice dripped with mockery, his eyes glinting with a dangerous mix of amusement and contempt, "Oh great false king who cast all aside, even the very life of your beloved. It's time we settle things." His eyes darkened.

Leona's eyes darted between the two men, her heart pounding. The tension was suffocating, the very air heavy with the promise of violence. She wanted to speak, to do something, anything to stop what was about to happen, but her body was frozen, paralyzed by the weight of her father's anger and Felle's provocation.

Cyrus's gaze remained locked on Felle, his fury now a cold, controlled burn. "You speak of her as if you care," he said, his voice dangerously low, "yet you took her along with my knight. Only to return after cursing her and corrupting them both."

Felle's smile widened a predator's grin. The blade in his hand hummed with power, black lightning crackling along its edge, eager to be unleashed. "Cursed her?" he echoed, his tone mocking. "You misunderstand, Cyrus. The only curse I bear is that of a future you created without Vyes. Your lies led your daughter to the ruins underneath this forest, and the consequence of those stolen relics befell her. But she chose to walk this path with me—willingly to hear the truth for herself."

Leona's heart twisted at his words, torn between the truth in them and the fear of the storm brewing between these two titans. She had indeed chosen this path, but now, standing between her father and Felle, the gravity of her choice was crushing.

Cyrus raised his sword, the tip pointing directly at Felle. "Then let her witness the consequences of that choice," he said coldly. "Cease to be before her eyes."

The ground beneath them trembled as both men prepared to unleash their power, the air around them crackling with energy. Leona finally found her voice, desperate and trembling.

"Stop!" Leona cried out, her voice trembling with desperation as she stepped forward. The crackling energy whipping through the air lashed out, knocking her small frame back. She hit the ground hard, but determination surged within her, more potent than the pain.

Felle turned his head to meet her eyes, a fleeting softness in his gaze before it hardened again. "I told you I would do as I must." His voice was cold and unwavering. He tilted the sword in his hand, his focus returning to Cyrus.

A resounding boom echoed through the forest as the two charged at each other, their movements a blur of steel and fury.

Leona's heart raced as she watched them clash, the sound of metal against metal reverberating through the air. Before she could react, she felt a strong arm wrap around her waist, pulling her away from the battlefield. Dean's grip was firm, and he moved quickly, guiding her away from the chaos unfolding around them. Knights lay scattered among the rubble and dirt, their bodies still from Felle's earlier assault.

"No! I must stop this!" Leona screamed, pounding her fists against Dean's chest as hot tears streamed down her face, shame and helplessness tearing at her.

Dean didn't look at her, and his jaw clenched as he continued to pull her away. "You can't, Leona." He hesitated, then spoke with a pained resolve, "We have to focus on your curse." His voice softened as he finally met her tear-filled eyes, his gaze clouded with worry and anguish.

They came to a halt as a massive explosion erupted behind them, its force sending shock waves through the ground. Dean instinctively shielded Leona, his body tense with fear. Smoke filled the thick and suffocating air as lightning crackled around them, racing towards the castle gates.

Leona broke free from Dean's hold, her heart pounding. She wiped the tears from her face, her breathing ragged as she steadied herself on the forest floor.

"How can I focus on that when they're killing each other?" Leona screamed at Dean in anguish and heart-wrenching panic. Dean's hands clasped Leona's face to calm her. "We have to find a way." His eyes were sincere as he spoke calmly to her amid the chaos around them. Another thunderous shock rang out as the two battled. Fear stirred within her with every sound. Leona snapped her head around. She was disoriented from the battle and the smoke surrounding the forest; amid her daze, her eyes caught the glint of metal from the corner of smoke.

In an instant, parting the smoke. A sword gleamed, slicing through; Dean forced Leona to the side as he met the blade with his own. Steely eyes greeted him—a twisted smile on a man's face consumed with malice. The man before them was the same dark-haired knight of the king's guard who set the flames in Siren. Rowan.

Dean quickly countered the knight as he swung with reckless precision, slicing through Dean's arm. He redirected his blade in a spray of blood, which blocked him from advancing towards Leona.

"Run!" Dean yelled through gritted teeth as he was locked in battle with the king's guard. "I do so enjoy a chase while hunting." Rowan's cold laugh caused chills to run down Leona's spine. Mars let out a hiss as the fur around her back stood on end.

"I will relish the fear in her eyes." Rowan's cruel smirk made him all the more unnerving.

"I'll kill you," Dean forced him back.

Suddenly, the forest erupted. Trees splintered and crashed to the ground as dark figures on horseback burst through the foliage, their armor glinting ominously in the dying light. These were not ordinary knights—their armor bore the crest of Aims king's guard, adorned with weapons yielding a dark aura. Their dull eyes and white hair were stark against their skin as they led their attack against the Lost Forest Kingdom. Leona began running toward the center of the battlefield, where her father was locked in battle with Felle. Mars closed the distance between them quickly.

Dean was still locked in battle with the other knight.

A loud reverberating crash and flash of lightning obscured everything from view. When Leona's eyes adjusted, the battle-field was awash with blood and violence. Her eyes frantically searched for any sign of her father or Felle. The sea of crashing forces was not easily discernible.

The walls of the kingdom had begun to crumble as the forces of the enemy knights continued their assault, spearheaded by the two white-haired knights Leona saw in Siren.

From the corner, a knight charged after Leona, still disoriented from the war zone in front of her. Mars leaped in front of her, preparing to provide an opening for Leona's escape.

White flashed in front of her as the knight was propelled backward. Leona snapped her head around, her mouth agape with shock and fear. Her eyes found her father in the distance, blood pouring from various cuts on his body. Inky black tendrils began coursing throughout the ground like the roots of a tree, wildly ripping through the ground and throwing the kingdom knights amongst the battlefields.

Caillte knights continued to pour out from the forest as they engaged the kingdom knights. Mars bit the leather flap on

177

Leona's boot and began tugging her forward; Leona was pulled from her shock and followed Mars toward the castle gates, now once again in full view. The chaos around them was like a wave of crushing steel and blood.

Cyrus continued commanding the knights into the fray as they fought the onslaught, and the power struggle continued.

For the moment, Felle and Cyrus had ceased their death match to dispel the forest invaders. Leona continued her pace to the castle as loud shocks emanated around her. Her eyes caught the sight of swirling black; in the middle of the fray, Leona spotted Felle, adorned with his cursed crown and the same sword coated with crackling black lightning as he continued his fight against the barrage of knights invading.

Then, the gleam of a massive sword crackled with white energy and pointed directly at Felle. Without hesitation, the knight barreled forward, aiming to strike down Felle. The knight had materialized out of the air itself. Leona felt an icy panic wash over her as she realized who had attacked Felle. It was the same knight Dean had just been locked in battle with so she could run.

Felle barely had time to react. He spun around, his blade meeting the knights with a loud clang that echoed through the forest. The impact sent a shock wave through the air, forcing Leona to stumble backward, her heart pounding in her chest.

Rowan callously countered, piercing through one of his own kingdom's nights as he continued his pursuit of Felle.

Chaos continued to descend upon the battlefield. The Kingdom of Aims knights swarmed the clearing outside the castle gates, their swords slashing through the air with deadly precision. Leona watched in horror as the knights closed in, their numbers too great, their power too overwhelming.

Despite his skill and fury, her father was pushed back, his white robes stained with blood, his sword dripping in it. Felle, his strength formidable, was having the tide of the battle turned against him as the knight continued his relentless assault, each contact creating a more considerable disparity in power reckoning throughout the forest.

In the midst of their power struggle, Leona's eyes looked on in horror. Without so much as a moment passed, a knight broke through the line, his sword arching toward her. Leona raised her hands instinctively, a burst of magic forming too late in her palms.

The blade struck her, piercing her side, as she cried out. Mars cried out in horror next to her.

Inky black tendrils skewered the knight who had pursued Leona. Blood poured from the holes left in his armor. Leona returned her gaze to the edge of the gates where Felle was fighting the knight Rowan.

Leona felt all senses begin to fade around her as she watched with tear-filled eyes. Felle's hand was outstretched towards where she was, where he had saved her from the knight. His flawless face looked straight at the knight who had pierced him with his sword. Blood began to pour from Felle's lips as the sword he had gripped in his hand started flicking away into embers, along with the black tendrils resonating throughout the battlefield.

Rowan pulled his blade from Felle's chest and kicked him to the ground, a cruel smile on his lips as he turned his gaze to Leona from across the clearing.

Tears streamed down Leona's face; she fell to her knees against the forest floor as she felt the warmth of her blood flowing onto the soil. A pulse rang out deep within her; the necklace Felle had given her was beginning to crack more, and the liquid started seeping through.

She could feel something stirring deep within her, a power she had long forgotten, buried deep within.

She closed her eyes with trembling hands and reached forward, hyper-focused on a singular thought that echoed throughout her being. *"Protect those dear to me."* The words echoed loudly in her head as thrumming began beneath her skin.

"Mars, take care of things," she whispered, a bittersweet smile tugging at her lips as fresh tears rose before Mars could respond.

A golden light, radiant and vibrant like the soft rays of daylight, began to pulse from Leona, growing brighter and more intense with each passing second. The screams and clashing of forces from the battle echoed in her ears, but it felt distant, drowned out by the roaring power building inside her.

The light erupted from her in a brilliant flash, blinding in its intensity. The energy surged through her veins, overwhelming and familiar. She felt the grip of the thorns that wound up her body, the curse that had bound her, its dark tendrils unraveling and flicking away like embers from a dying flame under the force of her newly awakened power.

Leona shakily rose to her feet, her body enveloped in the golden light. The smoke around them parted as the light expanded, pushing back the darkness that had consumed the battlefield. She raised her hands, and with a single, determined thought, she directed the full force of her power toward the battlefield before her.

The golden light brightly enveloped her.

A wave of heat and energy rippled through the forest, and with a deafening roar, the clanking of metal paused for a moment as shockwaves of light rang out in all directions.

Leona's breath came in heavy gasps, her heart racing as the curse's last remnants faded. For the first time in years, she felt free and unburdened.

The golden light around her dimmed, settling into a soft glow that radiated from her skin. The golden light crystallized into points at the tips of her ears. Her eyes bore the same otherworldly essence as Felle's, a mark of her awakened power.

The air around her buzzed as she parted the battlefield to where Felle was slumped against the earth, blood still pouring from his wound and down the sides of his lips. The knight Rowan had slipped back into the tree line along with the white-haired knights who had led the fray, leaving behind countless numbers of their own knights to die at the ends of the forest they invaded.

In the distance, Cyrus stood in stunned silence, injured from the battle, as the knights began pushing the forces out of the tree line.

Leona gently pulled Felle to her. His blue eyes were dim, his pale skin awash with the blood that had escaped his lips and flowed around him on the forest floor. Leona's emerald eyes, now bearing the same ethereal mark as the Fae met Felle's, slowly he, raised his hand to her cheek with his remaining strength, gently touching the side of her face where hot tears streamed.

His hand was slick with his blood. Felle's vision blurred as he looked at her.

"Y-you're...finally...awake..." he uttered breathlessly as his breathing began to weigh heavier on his chest. Leona gently clasped his hand and put hers against the gaping wound of the sword that marred his flesh. Blood pooled around him as Leona skidded next to Felle, her eyes wide with panic. She tried to staunch the bleeding, her hands trembling as she pressed down on the wound, but the blood kept coming, staining her fingers red.

A soft golden light began to weave particles into his skin. Felle's tired eyes slowly began to flutter closed as Leona continued to focus every ounce of power she had on sealing the wound. She was so focused that she did not immediately register the warm hand that Cyrus had placed on her shoulder at one point before departing once again. Leona was unsure of how much time had passed; the glow that had illuminated her fingers slowly began to recede. Her emerald eyes were still wet with tears. She felt her breath catch as Felle slowly opened his eyes, meeting Leona's.

The wound on his chest had closed.

Leona felt her lip begin to quiver as she fell forward onto Felle and began to cry. He let out a groan before gently patting her back as she heaved tears into him.

Cyrus's voice echoed behind Leona as he continued his efforts to command the knights who continued their pushback against the lingering men from the Kingdom of Aims.

"Leona?" Dean's voice uttered in disbelief; hearing the familiar tone pulled her from her tears; she turned to see Dean standing behind her, gripping his side where blood was slowly trickling, a pained expression present on his face.

She met Dean's gaze. Upon seeing her, his eyes wide with shock and disbelief. He reached out to her, and she took his hand, pulling her to him as he tightly embraced her. Her crimson hair wildly fell around her, dried blood-soaked and streaked her pale skin, and her otherworldly eyes filled with tears once again.

"It's over," she whispered, her voice filled with newfound strength.

Dean's eyes filled with tears as he embraced her tightly once again. The battle around them had all but stilled; Cyrus stood near the edge of the clearing, his eyes troubled as he reluctantly closed the distance between him and Leona. Dean untangled himself from Leona as Cyrus approached.

His silver hair was streaked with blood; blood stains and the markings of a fierce battle marred his usual regal appearance. Cyrus averted his gaze. A look of uncertainty clouded his face as though he was afraid Leona would shatter at any moment.

"Are you okay?" he asked Leona curtly. Leona looked at him; a look of sadness washed over her.

"I'm fine," Leona uttered. She parted her lips as though she would speak, but before any words escaped, Cyrus crushed her against him in a tight embrace. Leona's eyes were wide with shock.

"I'm so sorry," the words fell from his lips, sincerity clear in his tone. "I never wanted you to know the sting of war or to become a part of it. I should have told you everything so long ago." Cyrus's gray eyes looked upon Leona, pleading for her to understand. "Then tell me now." Leona softly countered. Cyrus tightened his embrace,

"I'll tell you everything." Leona gave into his embrace as she heard the words.

Dean slumped down beside where Felle lay, still recovering from his injuries. His hand was still firmly grasped against his side. Dean met his gaze, "You look like crap," he uttered.

Felle felt a weak smile pull at his lips as he observed Dean, "I still...look better than you..." he paused between breaths. Dean felt a pang of relief hearing Felle quip back with his sarcastic jabs.

Cyrus released her, his hands lingering for a moment. Leona turned toward Dean, who was slumped against a tree near Felle, exhaustion etched on his face.

She knelt by his side, and soft light began to glow from her fingers once again, this time slowing the trickling of blood that was streaming from Dean's side.

Dean breathed a heavy sigh of relief as he felt the pressure ease on his wound. Leona lowered her hands and gave a thoughtful look at the forest she knew better than herself. The devastation from the battle was sobering. The trees were splintered and destroyed in large areas, the ground was torn apart, and rubble was scattered throughout. The battle between the Kingdom of Aims and Caillte left many casualties of war strewn about the land.

The Castle gates were all but destroyed, splintered wood and stone scattered across the ground. Some of the forest mages were caught in the crosshairs of the violence, they stood amongst the wreckage, faces grim and bloodstained.

Leona felt a heavy weight upon her chest as she considered the vast devastation. With the king's guard nowhere to be found, she could only assume they had slipped away from the battle during the chaos.

"You broke your curse, Leona," Mars cooed as she rubbed her face upon Leona's leg. Leona pulled Mars into a tight embrace. "We finally made it home, Mars" Leona smiled through her tears.

22

A Promise

The sun shone brightly in the sky, and the forest was quiet as the wind gently tousled the leaves. Two days had passed since the battle shook the lost forest and the mages within it. The lingering touch of war had embroiled the forest in a quiet frenzy, the fear of uncertainty was teeming within those who called the inner walls home.

Leona gazed at herself in the mirror of her room, the same one she had looked upon the day this had all begun.

The face looking back was much different than the one she saw before. Her wild crimson hair flowed around her in twisting waves, her pale skin took on a glimmering sheen, and her emerald eyes maintained the otherworldly characteristics of the Fae.

Her ears no longer held the crystallized light particle tips she bore while using all her magic. Once the battle had ended, they slowly flickered away into embers of soft light.

She looked at her wrist, where the curse mark of thorns once lay etched into her skin. Her pale flesh bore no sign of ever having it. After the battle, her father stayed true to his word and revealed everything to Leona.

Cyrus had detailed the events of the past to Leona, from the first war a century before to the truth behind the Lost Forest and the magic that teemed within it. Leona had listened intently as Cyrus told her about the first grimoires that were given to his father's father as an act of goodwill to the humans of Caillte, who sought a peaceful world free of the oppression of the kingdom's regime and hatred of magic.

Leona had looked at her father in shock and awe as he explained the past.

"Tell me about her," Leona had asked Cyrus; he gave a wry smile,

"Twenty years ago, I set out alongside my younger sister to seek the aid of the Fae who had given us the gift of magic a century earlier. The gift that had spurned the first war. We wandered the land, lost and uncertain of the humans outside the forest. As we searched for the forbidden lands where the Fae resided, humans tricked us into a nearby village. The Kingdom of Aims sent knights to attack us; in the heat of battle, I was wounded, and we were separated as we were forced to flee into the nearby forests. I managed to escape my pursuers, but I was mortally wounded. I found a clearing in the woods that I thought would be an excellent place to slip into eternity, and as I lay there, the strangest thing happened." Cyrus paused for a moment as he fondly recollected the memory. "A woman with crimson hair and emerald eyes appeared as if from thin air. She asked me what had happened, and I told her, "I was on a journey with my sister when the knights attacked us." She took pity on me and attempted to treat my wounds; as we spoke, she asked me what was worth risking my life for, and I told her the truth. "To find those who gave us the gift of magic because I wanted to stop the war and live in peace." The woman smiled kindly at me before disappearing. I thought she was a dream, something comforting to take with me into the next life.

To my surprise, she returned, this time with a strange knife; she spoke an incantation and used her magic to bind her life force to mine. A thread that could not be seen bound us to one another. Shortly after she healed me, my sister happened upon us, and we all returned together to Caillte.

She reinvigorated the forest; she taught the mages so much. With her help, we were able to turn the tides of war, and an armistice was passed between us and the non-magic realm, forbidding magic outside the walls of the forest. Three years had passed in the blink of an eye, and your mother was nearing the end of her life. Had I known that the cost to save me that day would be her undoing, I would have gladly welcomed the embrace of death. She would not hear it," Cyrus's gray eyes were filled with sad nostalgia as he looked at Leona. "She said that our love and the life we created was proof that her wish for a world with peace could be true." Leona felt tears prick her eyes.

"Why did you let her die?" Leona uttered her voice barely a whisper.

"It was never up to me," Cyrus spoke softly.

"You could have saved her! You could have let her go back with him!" Leona shouted as tears stung her eyes.

"It was never up to me, Leona," Cyrus looked at her through eyes laced with sadness.

"She could've been here...I could've seen her face..." Her voice was as soft as a whisper, as the tears streamed from her emerald eyes.

"You are so much like your mother was," Cyrus began before Leona cut him off.

"Why are there no portraits or traces of my mother here?" Leona asked Cyrus while averting her eyes.

He hesitated, and an uncomfortable silence settled between them.

"I couldn't bear to see her face or to relive the memories of the time I had with her," Cyrus replied, broken. His gray eyes remained averted from Leona's as he continued.

"For a long time, I could not even look upon you; you bore such a striking resemblance to her. Every time my eyes caught sight of your crimson hair and emerald eyes, I was reminded of hers." guilt was plain across his face as he uttered the words. Leona felt a wave of relief after hearing the words from his lips; for so much of her life, she had lived with the ingrained belief that she was the failure of the royal lineage. In all actuality, she was the sole living reminder of a future that had survived in the face of persecution.

"No wonder I was always alone," Leona uttered the words softly, a sad smile playing across her lips. Cyrus gave her a thoughtful look and finally raised his eyes to meet hers, his silver hair cascading in tousles around his mature face.

"I have made countless mistakes." he gripped the edge of the leather couch they had sat on. "Acted with only self-interest, completely consumed in creating the peace I fought so long for," he gave Leona a defeated smile, "I'm truly pathetic," he softly laughed to himself.

Leona could feel the weight of the conversation settling heavily into her bones. Despite everything that she had endured, the loneliness she had known for so long, the internal conflict, and the weight of being a failure. All of these things seemed to pale in comparison to the feeling she had seeing how broken her father truly was in the wake of bearing the responsibility of the kingdom, even at the cost of those he loved. For all of the power he held, he had no way of using it to protect what he cherished most.

Leona instinctively reached for the necklace that Felle had given her before realizing its absence once her fingers trailed only her skin in its place. During the battle, it had all but fallen apart. Her awakening caused the vial to shatter completely. The tattered remains of it lay on the nightstand inside her chambers, serving as a reminder of how far she had come and as a comfort close to her while she slept.

Leona gave her father a knowing look as she gazed at the man. His intimidating presence was replaced by slumping shoulders and the marks of age elegantly etched into his features.

"I forgive you." Her voice was calm; it did not shake. Leona was not sure she entirely meant the words that she had spoken to him; the deep hurt that burned inside of her still seared within; despite that, she could not bring herself to add to her father's suffering. Seeing how broken he was reminded her a great deal of Felle. No matter how many years have passed, they both remained frozen, haunted by the past and the pain of losing what they held most dear.

Cyrus broke the silence between them.

"The ruler of the forbidden lands came here once, demanding we return her. I hated him. Because he represented everything she lost and everything I could not give her." Cyrus's words were sincere; Leona was shocked at her father's honesty; she had never known him to be so open.

"Do you still hate Felle?" Leona asked after a moment; Cyrus gave her an exasperated look. "You speak his name so familiarly; please do not break your father's heart again and tell me you wish to be away with him." His eyes were pleading. Leona was taken aback as she felt embarrassment well up inside her. She averted his gaze, a blush apparent on her cheeks.

"It's not like that," she corrected shyly.

Cyrus let out a worried sigh.

"Leona, despite what you may think, Felle is not someone to be taken lightly. He is dangerous." Cyrus spoke with a curt tension to his voice.

"Once his injuries have healed enough, he will be expelled from this forest once more." Cyrus's voice was unwavering. Leona gave him a sullen glance.

"I guess you do still hate him." She uttered, annoyance clear in her tone. Cyrus's silver hair cascaded loosely around him, and his regal face was pulled into a grimace as he sighed.

"Hate would require your father to have a conscious thought, and I can assure you he doesn't," the mocking voice rang out from the door to the great room Cyrus and Leona had been speaking in. Against the corner of the door, Felle braced himself, a look of mischief and malice across his usually emotionless face; his black tunic hung on his slender frame, and his eyes remained sharp as they fixed on Cyrus.

Anger erupted from Cyrus as he tensed, walking in front of Leona to cover her from Felle's gaze. "Since you can stand, you can leave my forest." Cyrus huffed, glaring intently at Felle.

"Father!" Leona gave him an incredulous look. Cyrus's face deepened into a scowl.

Felle met his gaze steadily, his expression unreadable. "Why would I leave the forest when Leona is here?" his cool reply incensed Cyrus, who tensed his posture as he faced the man head-on.

"Why would I allow you to live when you have already caused so much harm to her." Cyrus glared menacingly at him. Felle regarded him for a moment before easing his stance.

"I have yet to harm her, nor do I have any intention of harming her," Felle paused for a moment, his blue eyes narrowed at Cyrus, "nor do I desire to slay you in front of her." His calm voice seemed to only further the tension between the two men.

Finally, Cyrus slowly stepped aside, though his gaze remained locked on Felle. "If you so much as..." He hesitated, his eyes threatening, "There will be no place in this world or the next where you can hide from me."

Cyrus and Felle exchanged a long, loaded look. Their tension was far from resolved, but it would seem other matters occupied their attention for now.

Leona was dumbfounded by the interactions between the two. She had never heard her father speak like this to anyone. Seeing him outside his usual regal persona was odd enough; however, watching him and Felle interact was truly painful and awkward, to say the least. Felle caught her glance and continued to stare after her even as she turned to avoid his gaze. Leona knew Felle enjoyed making others uncomfortable, but she had no desire to play these games in front of her father, of all people.

A soft knock at the door pulled Leona from her thoughts and the memories of what had transpired within those two days. She turned her attention from the mirror where she had recounted the events of her father. The rosewood door gently opened, revealing the stark black tousles of Dean's hair. His eyes were bright as he met Leona's.

"Dean!" she collided with him. He hesitated before allowing her to give way to his embrace. After a moment, Dean pulled Leona away from him and gave her a soft smile.

"I guess Felle and Cyrus haven't killed each other yet," he teased with a laugh. Leona let out an exasperated sigh, "Somehow, I feel like that won't last long," she uttered as she thought about the two men tensely shooting daggers at each other whenever they happened to lock eyes. Dean's fingers lightly trailed over one of Leona's rebellious locks of crimson hair, and he met her eyes again.

"Leona, I'm sorry for everything." His voice was soft as he spoke to her. Leona's eyes focused on Dean; she gently regarded him,

"I'm not," her voice did not waver. "If it weren't for the curse, I don't think I ever would have known the truth," Leona spoke with a confidence that she had never known. Dean parted his lips as he found himself lost in Leona's emerald eyes; although they no longer bore the same human characteristics he had always known, he couldn't help but feel entranced by them.

"You've become so strong." His eyes never left hers as he spoke.

"I was tired of running," she spoke softly.

"Leona, I—" he paused momentarily. "Do you remember when you turned fifteen, and your father forbade us from seeing each other?" His eyes held a quiet intensity.

"He was upset that I had snuck away from my chambers instead of continuing my royal lessons with Yara." Leona recollected

"Do you remember what I told you that day when you saw me under the trees?" his voice was so soft and sincere. Leona's eyes widened as you recollected. Before she could speak, Dean

192

gently tucked a crimson strand behind her ear.

"I told you that whether it was this life or the next, you would never face anything alone." His words were sincere as his eyes searched hers.

His hand gently clasped her face as he leaned forward and softly placed his lips against hers. Her breath caught in her throat as she parted her lips against Dean's. Leona had never imagined Dean could feel this way for her; her mind raced as she considered everything that had transpired between them. Dean gently pulled his face from hers and allowed his hand to fall from her cheek. Leona averted his gaze, and she began to blush.

"I meant what I said that day and still mean it." Dean gave her a wry smile before turning and approaching the door, "By the way, Mars was looking for you," he uttered. "She was in the throne room." Dean shut the door behind him. Leona gave one last thoughtful glance to herself; for the first time, she did not see the same weak girl gazing back at her.

Leona's steps were light as she followed the winding halls to the throne room. Mars had made herself scarce since the battle. Leona's thoughts were running rampant as the memory of Dean's lips pressed against hers flashed in her mind; her fingers instinctively touched her lips. She could feel the heat return to her cheeks once again.

What would Mars think when she told her, she wondered. What was Mars thinking these days? Leona was worried that she may have been injured or, perhaps, she may have been angry at her. The large carved door opened slightly as Leona slipped inside.

Her mouth was agape as she saw the throne room. The

flowers were all blooming, creating a cacophony of colors and soft textures lining the stone walls. The small stream seemed more lively than usual, and the throne's carved marble lay vacant except for the diminutive black cat that resided in it.

"Mars!" Leona exclaimed as she closed the distance between them. Mars met her eyes and gently stumbled to a stand. "Leona!" Her voice was soft, and there was a hint of something underneath. Leona regarded her with a worried expression as she knelt beside her from where she stood in front of the throne.

"What's wrong?" Leona questioned her gently. Mars's green eyes filled with tears.

"I am so grateful to you, Leona; you have allowed me to stay by your side for all these years." Mars gently inched closer, rubbing her face against Leona. Leona embraced her, "We'll always be together!" she assured her.

"Leona," Mars paused momentarily, still in Leona's embrace. "I've been able to stay by your side because of a promise I made the day you were born to your mother." Mars softly uttered. Leona's eyes widened in surprise, "As a familiar, I swore a sacred promise to Vyes, a promise that tethered me to this world and to you." Leona slowly lowered Mars from her chest and met her eyes. Confusion began to well up inside of her.

"I don't understand, Mars; we're always going to be tethered to each other." Leona asserted, confused. Mars's large green eyes filled with tears, "Thank you for allowing me to keep the promise," Mars softly cooed. Leona felt panic writhe within her as a soft glow emanated from Mars.

"What promise? What's happening?" Leona cried out; hot tears streamed down Leona's face as she saw flecks of black particles begin to flick away into soft embers.

"My promise was to stay by your side until you could stand

on your own." Tears fell from Mars's eyes as she began to dissolve before Leona. Leona pulled her tightly to her chest; realization washed over her as she understood what this meant. The embers did not cease. "Keep moving forward, Leona," her soft voice cooed as the last particles dispersed into golden flicks of light that disappeared into the atmosphere before her. Leona crumbled into a mess of tears and screamed as her heart wrenched. She lay, writhing in heartbreak as the doors swung open and the soft hand of her servants tried to soothe her. All reason had left her as she crumbled.

"Mars!" Leona cried out.

Leona was inconsolable as the days passed. A deep longing resonated within her; Mars was all she had ever known for as long as she could remember. Leona felt hopeless and lost; there was so much of this world she did not know, and her father could not provide her with a shred of solace. Felle tried to comfort her by telling her that Mars had not perished but had instead returned to where spirits resided outside the living realm.

Dean had tried to console her; he held her tightly in his arms as he gently caressed her hair, but Leona had felt utterly numb to his endeavors of comfort. Mars consumed her thoughts, and her words echoed in Leona's mind.

Without so much as a goodbye, she could only hear the soft utterance of "keep moving forward." Leona could not fathom how to continue forward when her heart was in pieces, and her mind was too busy to think. Mars gave her the courage to continue forward; even if she had not always realized how profound it was, she was now conscious of the ways in which Mars was always guiding her and leading her toward her destiny.

From the times she when was a mere child and would sneak out of the castle, Mars was always next to her, urging her forward to Dean or the kind servants who would quietly escort her back to her chambers without alerting the palace guards or Yara of her escape. Mars had always guided Leona on her journey. She was there every step, supporting her even when they seemed to be at odds. Leona knew that there were no words that she could hear to bring her comfort, nor did she wish to hear them. She feared any comfort she found, would mean accepting a world in which Mars no longer exists, unchanging, and devoid of warmth.

Her tear-drenched eyes caught sight of a gleaming from her window.

The first light of morning was reflecting in her window. Leona opened the latch, throwing it open. She swung her legs over and out onto the side without a second thought. Her fingers lased the lattice of vines that led down to the ground below, and she began to climb down. Her crimson hair whipped freely around her in the gentle breeze, and her legs felt a prick of the morning chill as her simple black dress billowed in the wind.

The moment Leona's boot-clad feet hit the ground, she sprinted. Something in her was compelling her forward; she could not describe it. It felt like an invisible thread was pulling her along, with only the sound of the brush and twigs snapping beneath her steps on the forest floor as she tore through the dense woods.

Leona spotted a small fox from the corner of her eye; it met her eyes. Her footsteps stalled as the sun shone through the break in the trees. The fox seemed to beckon to her as if trying to communicate for her to follow. The creature's brown eyes looked intently at her before setting off toward the edge of the forest. Leona had no time to react; her feet began moving again, this time toward the fox.

She tore through the woods as she tried to close the distance between them; she was certain that this strange creature was beckoning her to follow, as every time it turned, the fox would pause in its strides until Leona caught back up. The fox jumped into the next corner of the woods; Leona followed until she crashed through a tree and directly into a wall. She reached out her hands to brace her, but her fingers did not graze the ground; instead, they were met with the soft touch of fabric.

Leona opened her eyes to her surroundings; a man with messy blond hair and golden eyes was below her, tangled on the forest floor. "Aver?" Leona mused, bewildered; his eyes softened as he recognized the woman who crashed into him; he propped himself up from the ground, "I've been looking for you." He met her eyes as he untangled himself from her and sat next to her on the forest floor. "You look different," Aver observed for a moment,

"Why are you here?" Leona questioned him, confusion evident in her voice. Without another word, Aver pulled out a messy bag, dumping its contents at her feet.

"This." Aver handed Leona a piece of parchment, which he grabbed from the pile at her feet. Leona looked at him perplexed as she began to smooth it out and examine its contents. Her eyes widened with curiosity and a question of confusion.

"A map?" Leona uttered as she continued studying it. A momentary pause gave way to a gasp of shock. "This is in Cailltian!" Leona exclaimed as she read the script. Aver gave her a hopeful glance,

"I knew you'd be able to read it. I found this along with the rest in a secret library hidden beneath the Kingdom of Aims." Aver's face gave nothing away as he continued. "And I think this might belong to you."

Aver pulled out a small leather-bound journal from the pile and gently offered it to Leona. Her emerald eyes immediately recognized the crest delicately etched into the side as the same one from her kingdom.

"This is the royal family's crest!" Leona parted the book and began to read the pages before her frantically. Her eyes filled with tears as she flipped through the pages, stopping at the inlaid portrait. Leona instantly recognized the regal face of the silver-haired man with his brilliant gray eyes as her father.

He looked no older than twenty, and her eyes found the crimson-haired Fae next to him, and her green eyes, the very same as Leona's, brought her to tears.

It was the first time she had seen a portrait of her mother.

Her neck bore an inky black thorn choker that was etched into her skin; the same pattern was shown on both her wrists, like cursed bracelets. Leona felt her breath catch in her throat as her eyes found the other woman in the portrait, her freckled face and long silver hair unmistakable; she knew instantly that this was Adira. Leona quickly put together the missing pieces; the sister her father told her of must have been the same sister who wrote in this journal.

Adira wasn't just the Siren's mage; she was her aunt and a member of the royal family of Caillte. Suddenly, it was as though it all clicked. She thought back to Adira, mentioning that she knew Cyrus and the forest and agreed to help Leona. It was because they were family. Leona met Aver's gaze,

"I thought she looked like you; I guess that means you're

part of the royal family. Right?" Aver quickly deduced Leona's lineage; Leona parted her lips,

"I'm supposed to become the ruler of Caillte," she softly uttered. Aver averted his gaze as a scowl pulled on his face.

"Of course," he let out a sigh. Leona gave him a sheepish look,

"Sorry," she murmured apologetically. Aver opened his eyes with a pained expression on his face,

"You may want to save that until after you've read this." He handed her a crumpled scroll, and Leona's fingers gently unraveled it, revealing a document stating the dissolution of the armistice between the kingdoms of the realm. Leona quickly snapped her head up and looked dumbfounded at Aver,

"What!" she gasped.

"Rowan and the kings' guard dissolved the armistice that bound the kingdoms in this flimsy treaty. After the forest, I went back to find them, and I stumbled upon a secret corridor under the castle that housed these people, but they weren't people; they were using them to create magic," he paused for a moment, "after I found these," he gestured to the pile of parchments before them, "I tried to speak to my father. Still, he was nowhere to be found; the castle was empty, aside from this declaration pinned in the throne room." Aver regarded her with a cautious curiosity as Leona began rifling through the parchment. Her eyes scanned each page until her hands tightened on one of the pages.

"What does it say?" Aver's voice held a quiet urgency..

"That the truth lies between this world and the next, inside a Forest of Forgotten Light." Leona's voice had an inclination to it.

"What do you mean this world and the next?" Aver questioned her; Leona's emerald eyes lit with determination. She pointed to a series of small islands marked faintly on the map, her voice barely a whisper: 'This must be it—the place between the realms of this world and the next.' She continued to examine it and spoke again, confident in her understanding.

"This is the place it talks about, between the kingdoms and the seas." Leona's eyes scanned the map, the lines and symbols coming alive under her gaze. A renewed determination washed over her.

"Mars might be there," She murmured, rifling through the pages as if they held the key to her hope.

"Who?" Aver questioned.

"My familiar, well, she wasn't mine, but she was a familiar." Leona began, "Felle said that the spirits of familiars don't perish; they just return to the land between the living and the after. That must be it." Leona pulled herself to her feet; Aver followed after her as she began to walk back into the dense woods; his hand pulled her wrist,

"Wait, Leona," he met her eyes as he closed the distance between them, his golden eyes peered at her, "I have no clue what a familiar is, but I need to go there; I need to find the truth. So I can put an end to Rowan." Aver spoke earnestly as he urged Leona to understand.

"I need to find Mars, and I can't let it end like this," Leona uttered as tears began to well in her eyes. Aver gently twined his fingers with Leona's and started walking back towards the edge of the forest.

"I can't read the script on the map, so we'll go together to this forest or eternity gate or whatever it's called." he pulled her along,

"But-" Aver looked at her over his shoulder,

200

"You need to find your friend, and I need to save my kingdom." Aver's eyes were dripping with sincerity.

"I know, but I can't leave without a word-" Leona began. Aver gave her a mischievous smile as he pulled her back to the tree line; he untangled his fingers from hers as he began rifling through the parchment that was left strewn about, pulling one from the pile along with a small quill pen. He offered them to Leona,

"Leave a note." Leona felt a smile pull at her lips as she grasped the small quill and began to write on the parchment. Once she was finished, Aver took a knife engraved with the Aims crest from his side and stabbed it into the tree, pinning the parchment in place. "Let's go," Aver offered Leona his hand; the morning sun shone brightly through the trees, illuminating him in soft light. She glanced thoughtfully at the forest behind her before taking his hand.

23

The Weight of A Promise

The forest buzzed with restoration, and the afternoon sun beat down heavily. Felle watched from atop the castle's window as the forest mages attempted to rebuild after the battle. He felt a pang of guilt as he thought about the familiar Leona so profoundly cared for. His blue eyes observed the bustle below as he considered everything that had transpired.

He was sure that war between the kingdoms had reignited after the battle, but the question in his mind was how to keep Leona out of it.

There was little chance that now that she was awakened, she would be willing to abandon the castle to return with him to The Isles, especially now that Cyrus managed to smooth things over with her.

His slender frame leaned back against the window, a pained expression on his face. His long black hair fell in waves around him.

Perhaps, he thought, if he spoke to Leona, she would consider abandoning this world now that Mars was no longer tethered to it.

He outstretched his legs as he dropped himself back inside the window. In a swift movement, he straightened himself. The tendrils of magic that had whipped out of his usual coat had all but torn it to shreds. All Felle had on were his fitted black pants and tunic, which clung to him tightly. His boots clicked against the stone of the castle's floors.

He found himself walking through the winding corridors of the castle. If he told Leona of the promise he made Mars, would she be more inclined to leave with him? He continued around the corner; the tall slats of the windows cast light along every surface. In the distance, his eyes found a rosewood door. He quietly closed the distance between the door and him and pulled it open.

The room was undoubtedly hers. The bed was unkempt; silk tapestries lined the walls, and a small nightstand in the corner caught his attention. On it, the crumbling remains of the necklace he had given to her in The Isles. His fingers gently trailed over it as a gentle breeze blew in, billowing the sun catcher that hung near her window. Vibrant glass pieces danced against the breeze from the open window as light cascaded through them.

"She's gone," Felle uttered to himself. A quiet wave of anger coursed through him as he peered out the window; on the grounds below, the knights were crowding. He perched on the window and jumped forward before hitting the ground below. Felle straightened himself as he approached. A flash of stark hair and blue eyes caught his attention.

"What are you doing, boy?" Felle asked Dean questioningly. Dean met his gaze, his eyes filled with fury as he gripped a tattered parchment.

"Leona left with that knight from Siren." He uttered through gritted teeth. Felle felt a cold wave of malice course through him as he approached Dean, grabbing the parchment from his hands to read it himself.

I didn't want to leave without a word, but I couldn't bear the thought of never seeing her again or of the kingdoms destroying each other and themselves. Don't follow me; Aver and I are going to set things right. I hope you can find it in your heart to forgive me once I've returned.

• Leona

Felle's blue eyes sharpened as rage flowed through him.

"Where did you find this?" Felle seethed, anger apparent in his tone. The knights led him to the forest's edge, where parchment was strewn. Felle knelt and began to tear through the pages; after a moment of riffling and scanning the contents, Felle gripped one of the pieces of parchment and straightened himself, his eyes intently burning every detail into his memory.

"I know where she went," Felle spoke sternly. Dean met his gaze, and the other knights murmured in anticipation. Felle gave Dean a questioning glance,

"She went to the Forest of Forgotten Light." Felle's words were laced with a quiet intensity.

Dean regarded the knights, "Go! Inform Cyrus now!" Without another word, Felle started towards the tree line; Dean followed behind,

"Where are you going? We must find Leona!" Dean exclaimed, annoyance clear in his tone. Felle's tense face looked down at Dean,

"Where do you think I'm going, you idiot?" He spat the words at him. Dean straightened, "I'm going to bring her home." Dean spoke each word with conviction. Felle let out a cold laugh. "You?" he met his gaze, "Perhaps reading isn't your strong suit; last I checked, your name was not inscribed as her adventure partner in her little note." Dean averted his eyes as he dug his nails into his skin, pained frustration apparent on his face.

"I get it, Felle. I know I'm useless. I know I'm weak. And I know that I probably won't be any help compared to you. But I need to go after her." Dean uttered the words through gritted teeth.

Felle met his eyes and held his gaze before speaking, "I think this is the first time you have had a slight conscious thought. You're right, though; you are completely useless compared to me." A cruel smile pulled at his lips. Dean straightened his posture and faced Felle, "Even so. I'm going,"

Felle let out an annoyed sigh and began glaring intently at Dean.

"You would only get in the way," he replied condescendingly.

"I'm going," Dean countered again. His eyes were unwavering as he faced Felle. After a moment of hesitation, Felle pushed the parchment into Dean,

"Fine. We leave now." Dean grasped the parchment as he followed behind Felle, making his way toward the human village of Tearn. "We don't have supplies-" Dean started before Felle shot him a warning glance,

"Shut up, you idiot." Felle pointed towards the cobblestone road that led to the human village ahead. A look of understanding crossed Dean's face as he realized what Felle was planning.

Dean examined the parchment in his hand and saw it was a written description of a place between the living realm and the after, between nations and the seas. It was not quite a map but a guide of sorts. Would this truly be enough to find Leona?

Dean gave a thoughtful look at the forest he had just left with Felle, before returning his eyes to the journey ahead. His sword affixed at his hip, the crest on his arm shone brightly against the sun, vowing only to return to the forest with her.

24

The Journey Ahead

The wind howled fiercely over the waves as the sun dipped below the horizon, surrendering the sky to the encroaching night. Leona's crimson hair streamed behind her like a banner, the last vestiges of daylight dancing on the waves. The shoreline was no longer in view. The vast expanse of the sea before them was all that awaited them for the next leg of their journey.

Leona's black dress whispered against her skin, the fabric catching the wind as her emerald eyes absorbed the deepening hues of twilight on the water. The ship Aver had led her to was one of the kingdoms, fully stocked for the knight's voyage. The large vessel cut through the seas as Aver steered it forward. Leona had read the directions of the map for Aver. She felt hope rise within her; even if she couldn't see Mars again, she could help Aver put an end to the senseless violence between the kingdoms.

As she watched him, Leona felt a strange sense of calm settle over her, mingling with the ever-present hope that had carried her this far. She had read the map's directions, guiding Aver with precision, but now, as the stars began to pierce the sky, she knew their true journey was only beginning. She might never see Mars again; even so, she had a duty to the realm and would not yield. Together, they could bring an end to the senseless violence that had plagued their world for so long.

Leona turned her gaze from the sea to Aver. The wind tousled his blond hair, his golden eyes fixed on the horizon, determined and unyielding. In the fading light, he looked every bit the hero she had once imagined in tales of old. His white shirt clung to his muscular frame, and the last rays of sunlight bathed him in a soft, golden glow.

"You should rest, Leona," Aver called out over the crashing waves, his voice gentle but firm. "We have a long journey, and who knows what lies ahead."

Leona met his gaze, her heart steady, her resolve unwavering. "I'm not afraid of what lies ahead," she replied, her voice soft but filled with quiet strength. "Not anymore."

Aver's laughter rang out, warm and genuine, cutting through the darkness like a beacon. His smile was a promise, bright and unwavering. "Then let's sail on, Leona. To the Forest of Forgotten Light, and whatever truth awaits us."

As the ship pushed forward into the night, the stars above mirrored the endless sea below, both vast and full of possibilities. Leona stood tall at Aver's side, her fears behind her, her eyes fixed on the future. Together, they sailed toward an uncertain path, the promise of a better world guiding them through the darkness.

At that moment, as the ship carried them onward, Leona

knew she was ready to face whatever pitfalls lay ahead. The journey was far from over, but she felt no fear, her resolve unwavering. The wind carried them forward, and with it, they prepared to face The Forest of Forgotten Light.

About the Author

Rin Ogawa is a passionate fantasy writer with a boundless love for storytelling and world-building. From an early age, she found joy and inspiration in the pages of any and all books she came across, this love sparked a deep desire to create fantastical realms of her own. Blending vivid imagination with fun, intricate plots, Rin crafts stories that transport readers to magical worlds where anything, even the impossible, can be possible.

When not writing, Rin enjoys playing the violin, creating artwork and exploring new literary worlds, and dreaming up new adventures. Armed with her favorite keyboard and boundless ideas, Rin continues to expand on the fantasy worlds inside her mind, bringing new life to them through her tales.

You can connect with me on:

🌐 https://rinogawa.com

🐦 https://x.com/RinWinsOgawa

www.ingramcontent.com/pod-product-compliance
Lightning Source LLC
Chambersburg PA
CBHW011517100726
47899CB00010BD/3398